LAVENDER FIELDS

NATALINA REIS

For information, contact the publisher, Hot Tree Publishing.

www.hottreepublishing.com

Editing: Hot Tree Editing

Cover Designer: Claire Smith

ISBN-10: 1-925448-97-5

ISBN-13: 978-1-925448-97-9

DEDICATION

To my son with love

FALLING
SKY

"What's happening?" I mumbled to myself. My mouth was parched and my eyelids, heavy as lead, struggled to open.

A sliver of bright light reached my eyes and I blinked rapidly, trying to force away the fogginess in my brain. Painfully slow, my eyes adjusted to the shock of the sudden brightness and fluttered open.

Was I dreaming or were there five pairs of round, flickering orbs floating above me? I blinked again and wiped what was left of my sleep-induced blurriness with my hand. Not orbs. Eyes. There were five pairs of eyes staring at me—three brown, one blue, but it was the fifth one that caught my attention. There was something odd about them. Not odd ugly, but rather beautiful like a pair of very rare gems. They didn't match. One was emerald green, the other a deep shade of violet. I had seen wind-whipped fields of lavender, but none as entrancing as the color mix of those eyes.

My hearing was coming back as well. I could hear their

hushed voices as they murmured to each other, wondering who or—more appropriately—what I was. It wasn't the first time something unexpected like this had happened to me. I was well known among my people as the klutz, the accident-prone one. My direct supervisor addressed me as "the liability."

"One of these days you're going to really mess up things for us all," he was known to say. As much as I would rather disagree, I couldn't. The truth was I was indeed a genuine klutz, someone who seemed to attract disaster and—worse, in my line of work—attention.

"What are you?" I heard a soft voice say. I blinked again and matched the voice to the owner of the strange pair of eyes. It was a male. Possibly in his mid- to late-twenties. In fact, now that my vision had cleared, I realized they were all young men, all staring at me curiously.

With a groan, I attempted sitting up, but my head spun and I fell onto my back again.

"Easy," the multicolored-eyed man said, reaching out to support me and help me up. "You must have bumped your head."

Had I ever! My descent had been abrupt, steep, and speedy. My body had picked up speed as it approached the ground, and even though I remember the fall into the beach, the second I hit the sand had ruptured my memory. That was by far my biggest fall ever.

The young man with the odd eyes slipped his hands under my arms and pulled me to my feet carefully. "There's no blood," he told me after checking the back of my head.

"I think you'll be all right."

I brushed my jeans and my black T-shirt, which were covered in sand.

"I'm Caleb," Mr. Lavender Fields said, offering a hand in welcome. "These are my friends. We were out for a walk on the beach and found you unconscious."

As I shook each of their hands, I studied them. They seemed to be in shock, almost in awe as they studied me in turn. I must have looked a fright, covered in sand and gravel—I seemed to have obliterated a big rock as I fell—as if I had been dumped on by a construction truck.

"Who are you?" the one called Caleb asked me. He seemed to be the only one who had fully functioning vocal cords.

"Sky," I answered, my throat scratchy from disuse. I hadn't used it in a very long time. I cleared my throat. "Thank you all for coming to my rescue." Even though, truth be told, I was in no need of rescuing. My kind did not get hurt in the human sense of the word.

"May I ask you what you are?"

Now that was a loaded and strange question. I looked like any other human. Maybe a little paler around my freckles, my blond hair streaked with more silver than in most people of my perceived age, but other than that I looked like a regular everyday human.

My eyebrow arched in question and I noticed his small pointing nod toward my back. Heavens! In the chaos of the fall, the loss of consciousness, and my general klutziness, I had forgotten to hide my wings. There they were, unfurled to their full glory, fluttering in the breeze like giant butterfly wings. Strike three for the clumsiest angel in Raphael's crew.

"Well…." *What exactly can I say— "I'm a freaking angel, deal with it"?* "I was trying out my new wings for the upcoming Comic Con." *Lying shouldn't come so easily for an angel.*

Judging by the relief on everyone's faces, I knew they believed me. All but Caleb, who was boring into my soul with those eyes.

"I don't believe it," he whispered for my ears only. I blinked and looked around, but the other men were moving away already, relaxed in the knowledge that I was just a regular geeky human.

"Well, it's true," I said, my lie weighing heavily on my conscience. An angel should never lie. Ever. But this was for a good cause. I couldn't out a whole race of creatures because I couldn't keep my flying speed under control, could I?

He pulled me aside, our backs—and now my retracted wings—to the others. "You're an angel." It was not a question. "I've seen one of your kind before."

So I wasn't the only clumsy angel in the realm. That was oddly comforting.

"What about you?" I asked, scanning his face for an answer. "Who has eyes like that?"

Caleb smiled. He had the sunniest smile I had ever seen. Something stirred inside of me. "Heterochromia. It runs in the family," he said with a soft chuckle. "Just a birth defect."

We sat down on a big rock, facing the ocean. "More like a gift," I said before I could stop myself. Why was I trying to impress this human with my silvery tongue? I had never been too flirty or too into the dating scene among my kind or humankind; as an angel, my proverbial plate was pretty full already with all my chores and responsibilities. Of course, we did get free time that theoretically could be used for romance, but I would have to stop making so many mistakes. My free time was spent mostly fixing my mess-ups, leaving very little time for fun.

The striking young man blushed at my comment, and my angel heart fluttered. How sweet was that?

"Is it hard?" he asked, his hand shyly inching toward mine on the rock between us. "To be an angel, I mean? What do you do exactly?"

"It's hard only when you're the biggest klutz in the history of Heaven like I am," I said, laughing and breaching the space between our hands. His was warm and soft underneath mine. Little electric shocks started with the contact and crawled up my arm. I had forgotten how nice this was.

His amazing mismatched eyes came to rest on mine, and my insides came alive with the force of a hurricane.

"What happened to you?" he asked, his voice lowering an octave, fingers interlacing with mine. "How did you fall? Are you a fallen angel?"

I'm falling for you. Seriously? What kind of magic was this human performing on me? I couldn't remember the last time I had feelings for anyone, and there I was quite literally falling for him.

"No, I'm just a regular angel here to collect a soul," I said, then immediately regretted it. Could I sound any creepier? Collecting souls?

"You're an angel of death?" He didn't look scared, merely intrigued. This one was a hard one to impress.

"Well, I guess so," I said, my hand itching to pull him closer. "On my way, I lost control of my speed and crashed." Because, as usual, I was going too fast.

"The souls don't mind waiting, Sky," Raphael always said. "They can wait. They're not going anywhere." But I had this superstitious streak that always feared the "other side" would get there first and collect the soul I was after. It didn't work like that, of course. You couldn't "steal" a soul. When a human died, their souls knew—even if their living bodies didn't—which way they were going. It was either up or down, and by that time it was too late to change the destination.

"How is it done? The harvesting of souls?" he asked, curiosity lightening his amazing eyes. "Do you have to watch them die like the Grim Reaper?"

That was too morbid even for this angel. "No, nothing like that," I explained. "We're given a list—sometimes with only one name, other times many. We get the name, place, time, and—so we're prepared—the manner of death. I try to get there as soon as possible after they pass so I can bring them the solace of Heaven as quickly as I can." In hopes the joy of a heavenly ever-after will compensate for the loss of loved ones.

Caleb was silent, his thumb playing havoc with my senses as he brushed it against the palm of my hand.

"I don't envy your job," he said. "You may be taking them to Heaven but also away from everything and everyone they've ever known or loved. It can't be easy."

He was right about that. "I've been trying for years to switch to the guardian angel patrol, but I'm too much of a screwup to elicit Raphael's trust. At least my charges are already dead. There isn't much harm I can do to them now."

Caleb laughed, then scooted closer to me. I sank against his heat, suddenly starved for his touch.

"Are angels allowed to date humans?" he asked suddenly, a faint blush spreading across his cheeks.

I looked around. Realizing the others had left us alone on the beach, I unfurled my white wings fully and, like a peacock, strutted them shamelessly. Then I tilted his chin up and kissed him, slowly and timidly at first, not sure of what his reaction would be. But his lips hungrily devoured mine. My angelic body turned to mush as his arms encircled my waist and pulled me against him. I buried my fingers into the silky folds of his black hair, drawing him closer. Folding my wings around us like a protective cocoon, I allowed myself a moment of total selfishness. I'd been an angel for a few hundred years, but I was certain I'd been created for that single moment in time.

I didn't want to go and, for a second, I considered handing in my resignation and becoming a mere mortal so I could spend a few years loving this human. His lips tasted of milk and honey, better than anything I had ever tasted before. I wanted to linger on them, savoring him, craving more of him. I wanted to lose myself in the lavender fields of his eyes. But of course I couldn't. Not right then. Not yet. I had a soul to collect.

I sighed, ending the kiss. "I have to go, Caleb," I said. "Souls to save and all that."

Caleb brushed his hand across my face in a tender yet electrifying caress. "Wings aside," he said, hot gaze meeting mine, "you are the most beautiful man I have ever met."

A silly smile stretched across my lips. "I'll be back," I whispered, standing reluctantly. "Give me your full name and I'll find you." I had Heaven's complete directory of living souls, after all.

"Caleb Pierce," he said, kissing me one last time.

With a great flap of my wings, I flew away, my heart already longing for Caleb's eyes. I would harvest my assigned soul and come back to his arms. I watched him from above as he waved at me and then walked the few yards to the beach's parking lot, climbed on his motorcycle, and drove away.

Taking a deep breath, I dug in my pocket for the name and address of the soul I was to harvest. The small piece of vellum was rolled into a tight little cylinder that I fought to unroll. I hoped I hadn't made the soul wait too long. It was five after six in the afternoon, and the sun was starting to descend into the ocean.

The vellum note held the deadly power of a dagger to my heart, for in it a lonely name had been scribbled in careless script. A name that a mere hour before wouldn't have held any particular meaning, but meant the world to me now.

Caleb Pierce, 6:10 p.m., Sunset Beach Ave, Motorcycle accident

***

TROUBLE

If you think angels never get angry, you've never met Gabriel. His face, normally peaceful and pale, was a visceral shade of red, and I could swear I saw smoke coming out of his ears. He leaned over, gripping the sides of his desk so fiercely I thought his knuckles were going to explode.

"You went too far this time, Sky." Spittle flew out of his mouth, and his eyes bulged out as if trying to escape their sockets. "It's bad enough that you have showered the Angelic Corps with all kinds of indignities thanks to a total lack of common sense or respect for our laws."

I'd had many tongue lashings in the past, but this one was turning out to be a real doozy. My face burned, though whether from shame or frustration I couldn't tell. I leaned back on my chair and my wings retracted on their own as if even they were afraid of this furious archangel.

"Twice in the past six months we've had to repair your broken wings. Twice." His voice was lowered to a threatening whisper. "Do you know how hard it is to repair angel wings? Do you know all that it involves? Of course you do. You just don't care." His voice, deceptively mild now, made me quiver in my shoes. "Three weeks ago, you practically caused a national panic when you were spotted flying low over Boothbay Harbor. What in Heaven's name possessed you to do such a stupid thing?"

I bit my tongue to prevent myself from answering. It was the thrill of the thing—the amazing feeling of the wind under my wings, the cold ocean air making my face tingle and my eyes water. It was exhilarating.

"Earlier this year, you were featured in the news in Portland as a UFO when you were reckless enough to hover over the bay during a full moon." I remembered that one well. My shock at seeing my glowing wings in a thankfully fuzzy photograph both in the newspaper and on television was quickly replaced by a sense of amusement. UFO indeed! I had been called many things before, but that was a first. Of course, Gabriel had not been amused.

"And now, the witch coven on Squirrel Island has been holding special ceremonies making offerings to the fallen angel they found napping on their private beach." His thin lips stretched even thinner, and his voice went up several octaves as he stared me down with those laser eyes of his. "Enough is enough, Sky. You're not a fledgling any longer. As a full-grown angel, you must be aware of our safeguards at every moment. They exist for a reason. They protect both the Corps and the humans."

With my head lowered for effect, I bit my lip again, not sure how I was going to get out of this one. Trouble seemed to follow me, I knew. I wasn't mischievous, just clumsy and a bit impulsive. Sometimes I wished there was some sort of ADHD medicine for angelic creatures so I could get a little help controlling my crazy instincts.

"And now the cherry on top of the ice cream," Gabriel said. "You go and save a human from his fate? Let me remind you what your job is, my son. You are an angel of death. You collect the souls of the departed and escort them to Heaven. That's it! You are not allowed to have a say in whichever fate befalls your charges. No choice at all. What made you think it was okay to prevent this man's death? What madness could have possibly crossed your weak little brain to make you do something so stupid? Answer me!" He was yelling now and, even though I didn't look, I was sure there were quite a few curious eyes and ears perking up behind the glass-like curtain that partitioned his office.

What could I say? That I had fallen in love with a mortal I didn't even know until a half hour before his death? That I couldn't bear the thought of losing him so shortly after I found him? That his eyes had me under a spell that rendered me incapable of intelligent decisions? After all, being an angel meant feeling everything hundredfold, stronger and faster. In spite of that, these answers wouldn't have gone down well with the enraged, and by now purple, archangel.

"What do you have to say for yourself?" He wouldn't stop until I said something. Anything. Not that he'd believe anything I said or that it would make a difference on how he felt about me and my actions, but he was used to being obeyed, and the fact that I was blatantly disobeying his order had to be chaffing him big time. "Speak!"

"It didn't seem right." My voice came out in a whisper. I was afraid of raising my eyes to him, so I kept them securely on my hands anchored on my lap.

"What did you say?" His voice boomed like thunder in the quiet of the night. "Speak up!"

I did raise my eyes then. Shaking inside, the familiar burn of injustice scorched my being. I was all about being fair and just. All angels were by definition. But we were also creatures bound by our own rules and by those who had authority over us. I had a lot of trouble following those rules sometimes. If anything remotely smelled of wrongdoing, I couldn't bring myself to do it. My whole being rebelled against it, and that's how I got myself in constant trouble. I had never done anything as serious as this though. For an angel in the death squad like me, saving the man I was supposed to guide into eternity was a huge no-no.

"Gabriel, I couldn't stop myself." I figured at that point honesty was probably the best policy. "It felt wrong. It felt horribly wrong to allow this young man to meet his fate so early in life."

The silence that followed my words scared me more than his yelling from before. It was never good news when Gabriel was quiet. I kept my eyes on him for fear of missing important cues in his expression or body language. Nothing. His eyes burned holes in mine, and I thought for a moment that his chest had started to inflate like a hot air balloon. This was not going to be pretty.

"He has so much to offer," I said to fill the silence. "We would be denying the world of his talents and promise."

Gabriel brushed a hand over his eyes and grunted. With a big thud, he dropped into his chair and took a deep breath. "There is no reasoning with you," he finally said, his voice almost back to normal. "You are confined to desk duty until further notice."

No, no, no. Desk duty meant I wouldn't be able to fly. Speed and flying kept me going. The only things I was good at, and the only time I felt truly free and in charge of my life.

"Isn't that a bit extreme?" Yeah, I wasn't very wise either.

The look Gabriel gave me could've melted metal. "I'm going to ignore that comment for my own sake." Could angels have a coronary? Because Gabriel looked ready to have one. "Get out of my office before I change my mind and send you straight up to the big boss. Maybe you'd like to explain to him why you went against his orders and made a mess of things."

I knew when I had overstayed my welcome. As quickly as I could muster on my seriously wobbly legs, I left his office and walked down the hallway, feeling the weight of everyone else's scrutiny. There would be nonstop tongue wagging at the dinner table tonight. Angelic Corps' headquarters was not your usual office building. The walls and floors were practically immaterial, and it wasn't a place where anyone could keep a conversation private. Since most angels followed orders without argument, the need for privacy was practically nonexistent.

And then there was me. The one who always stuck out like a sore thumb, who questioned everything under the sun, who found it extremely difficult to keep opinions to himself. Had they known there would be such a creature in their Corps, I'm certain they would've rethought the idea of gauzy walls and gone with real ones instead.

At the end of the walk of shame, my desk awaited. I had always liked my little corner; it was humble and out of the way, overlooking the great expanse of the sky below. On days when I was feeling particularly wistful, I would sit at my desk, looking out through my non-walls and imagining how fast I could fly through the fluffy, cold clouds beneath me. Today I dreamed of lavender fields and how those eyes had made me feel inside. I didn't even know you could feel like that. Angels are creatures raised to think of others rather than themselves, their mission above all else. It didn't normally leave much space or time for questioning their own feelings, their own dreams and wishes. Caleb had changed all that for me. His face was etched into my memory, and I knew that no matter what I did or what happened I would forever carry him in my heart.

I'm not sure how long I sat there, staring into the blue skies, going over each inch of his handsome face; every nuance of his dark, short hair; the promise beyond his unusual eyes. Warmth boiled to the surface inside me, and I was both happy and sad at the same time. It was a wonderful feeling, but it was scary as well. It had already gotten me in a heap of trouble.

When I read Caleb's name on my mission note, my heart had taken control over my brain. I flew the fastest I ever had to the site where he was to meet his demise, not quite sure of what I was about to do. In the end I didn't hesitate. I saw his bike as it careened around the curve, heading straight for a semi truck driving the wrong way. Before I even realized what I was doing, I plunged down in front of the truck and swept Caleb off his bike just as it fell and slid sideways under the giant tires.

"What did you do that for?" Caleb asked, surprised. I pointed to where his bike was nothing but a pile of mangled metal. "Fuck! You…. I…. Was I the soul you came to harvest? Am I dead?"

I laughed. A nervous chuckle as reality began to sink in. I had just saved the soul I came to take away. "You're not dead. I saved you."

Afraid of being spotted, I flew us to the first sheltered spot I could find and put him down gently.

"Are you supposed to do that?" His eyes were mesmerizing, and I found I couldn't take mine off them. I nodded, incapable of uttering a sound. "I thought you were supposed to take my soul to—well, hopefully Heaven. Why did you save me?"

I should've just flown away and hoped for the best. Instead, I grabbed his T-shirt, pulled him closer to me, and kissed him. This had to be some kind of seraphic madness for which I was in no hurry to find the cure. Caleb didn't fight me, raising his hands and threading his fingers through my curls while his tongue explored my mouth. Ambrosia. Pure, intoxicating ambrosia.

"This is madness." His breath caressed my lips, and I had to refrain from crushing him between my craving body and the wall behind him. "Am I dreaming, Sky? Hallucinating, maybe? You're an angel. A real, honest-to-God angel."

In the back of my mind there was a foggy idea of his earlier statement about having met another angel before, but the slow burning in my gut quickly convinced my brain to ignore it and focus on the task at hand. My hands had become a force to be reckoned with, moving of their own accord beneath his T-shirt, eager to explore every detail of his body.

It was indeed madness. I had just saved my charge. There would be hell to pay.

With that last thought, I came to an abrupt realization. I stopped my hands and detached my lips from his, breathless and suddenly anxious. I was in so much trouble. "As much as it pains me to say and do this, I have to go." I wanted to stay so badly. "I have to tell Gabriel what just happened. He's not going to be happy."

My eyes locked with his and I was flying over those sweet-scented fields again. My lips stretched into an uncontrollable smile.

"I don't know why you did it, but thank you for saving me," he said, sunshine taking over his face. I may be the angel, but he shone as if enveloped in a halo. "When will I see you again?"

Could I stay and ignore the call of responsibility? I wanted to. God, did I want it. But I knew I couldn't. Being an angel meant I wasn't free to do as I pleased. My life was not my own, and if I stayed, the Corps would find me one way or another. Easier to just go and face the music. At least

Gabriel wouldn't be able to accuse me of being a coward.

"Soon." *I hope*. I touched my lips briefly to his and then, unfurling my wings, I took off, heading upwards toward the clouds and the wrath of the angels.

STARTING AGAIN
FORGOTTEN

"Gabriel wants his coffee." Amy was giving me that look that said she was all too happy I was in the doghouse. She had never liked me. Or maybe she was a little scared of me. People were often afraid of what they didn't understand. Angels were no different.

I wanted to say, "Tell Gabriel to get his own coffee," but even I knew when to shut up. I stood up from my desk-turned-prison and dragged my feet all the way to Gabriel's office. The archangel was on the phone, whispering words I couldn't fully understand. Was he speaking in Seraphic? No angel used that language anymore. It was ancient, outdated, and only a very small number of angels could speak it. *Who is he talking to?* A terrible thought crossed my mind. *Is he talking to the big boss? Is he talking about me?*

As I walked in with the mug of steaming coffee, Gabriel rushed to say his goodbyes and pocketed the phone. "Finally! I thought I would have to open a branch of Starbucks in my office to get a cup." Gabriel fancied himself a witty angel. I handed him the coffee and turned to leave. "Wait a minute. I want to talk to you."

Obligingly I sat, my back straight, refusing to show my nervousness. "What do you want to talk to me about? Are you reinstating me into active duty?"

Gabriel laughed, dry and humorless. "By all the saints in Heaven, absolutely not!" *Figures.* "I wanted you to know that we have tried to fix your horrible lapse of common sense."

My heart flip-flopped in my chest. "What do you mean?" *Please tell me you didn't "cause" another accident.* "What did you do? Is Caleb all right?"

"He's fine." With a wave of his hand, he dismissed the idea. "We're angels, not monsters. Did you really think we would kill him?" *If I'm being honest, yes.* "We did pay him a visit, but only to repair some of the damage you caused by showing yourself to him."

Still not sure what he meant, and feeling the long fingers of anxiety beginning to stretch and close around my throat, I leaned forward in my seat. "What exactly did you do?" My voice came tainted with anger in spite of my best intentions to keep it cool.

Gabriel's smile died on his lips and his eyes hardened. "Relax. He came to no harm at all. And I suggest you stay away from him from now on. Not sure why you decided to do what you did, but it must end here. You've done enough damage already."

I left his office, chin on my chest, eyes on the floor. Some joker had printed and hung posters of me around the precinct. In the picture, I was holding a human in my arms and across the front, in big letters, it said, "How Not To Harvest Souls." I was used to being the butt of everybody's jokes, but it still stung. I didn't want to look at it anymore; I wanted to go home and crawl under my blankets and sleep until my time on desk duty was over. It had been almost two weeks since I was chained to that desk. I missed flying. I missed Caleb.

As the day went on, I allowed my anxiety to percolate inside of me, and by the end of the day it had reached the boiling point. I was angry too. Angry that I should be punished for doing what angels' general mission was: being merciful and loving. Since I couldn't fly, I ran all the way to my place on cloud nineteen. My residential cloud was reserved for those of… lesser worth. The screwups like me who kept making one mistake after another. I didn't care; my tiny little apartment was cozy and had everything I needed. At least it did until recently. Now I needed more. I needed Caleb beside me.

I paced around the small living room like a caged lion, finding some comfort in pulling on my shirt obsessively for lack of anything more constructive to do. What if I disobeyed my orders and sneaked down to Earth for a quick visit? I felt this inexplicable fear for Caleb's safety. Yes, I wanted to see him, to hold him against me and kiss him until my lips went numb. But most of all, I wanted to make sure he was all right. Gabriel's words still rankled, like a throbbing pain that wouldn't fade away. Instead it swelled to epic proportions. If my rugs hadn't been made of the finest divine thread, I'm certain I would've worn a hole in them with my incessant walking. My heart was galloping like a wild horse in my chest as panic replaced the nagging worry. *I have to see him!*

It wasn't dark enough yet to escape my block without being seen. My anxiety was so high I literally sat on my hands to wait. As soon as my room drowned in darkness I was off. Aware that I had to be cautious and avoid being caught breaking the rules again, I descended slowly—well, a lot slower than I normally would. Earlier in the week I had accessed the Corps' directory of souls and got Caleb's address. He lived in Wiscasset, a sleepy little town not too far from Boothbay Harbor, one of my favorite places to get in trouble, it seemed. I was surprised by that. It was an old town, full of historical buildings and a rather expensive place to live. Caleb couldn't be more than twenty-eight years old. I wondered what kind of job he might have to afford living in the quaint little town.

I alighted behind his house, in a small empty field which the night had rendered invisible. Retracting my wings, I walked slowly toward the front of the small cottage. The windows and front porch were brightly lit as I stopped for a moment to collect myself. *I must be careful.* I didn't know who else would be there, and I couldn't risk making any more mistakes. Heart aflutter, I knocked on the door, ignoring the bell on the side. I needed to feel something other than the crazed beating of my heart, and a little pain in the knuckles would do nicely.

The door cracked open and a face appeared from behind

it. It was not Caleb.

"Can I help you?" The young woman smiled kindly, and I lost my power of speech. Who was this little elfin girl opening my heart's desire's door? "Are you here about the cable service?"

Hell! Did I look like the cable guy? "No, I'm here to talk to Caleb." Regaining my voice, I decided it was best to go straight for it. "Is he here?"

The girl—for she looked barely out of her teens—turned her head around and called Caleb's name. "There's a guy here to see you." She turned back to me again, her eyes shining with mischief. "Are you his boyfriend?"

I opened my mouth to answer, but Caleb's voice beat me to it. "What are you going on about now, girl? Stop harassing every guy who comes to my door."

Our eyes met and I stopped breathing—well, I literally did. Angels can do that without hurting themselves. A wave of relief and something warm and gooey washed over me. "Hi, Caleb. Came to see if you were okay."

A quizzical smile curved the corner of his lips. "Excuse me? Who are you?"

A loud chuckle left my lips before I could stop it. "Funny," I said, stealing a glance at the young woman who was observing the exchange with great interest. "I was worried."

Caleb's eyes crinkled as he licked his lips. A tendril of heat ran through me at the memory of his taste. "I'm sorry, dude. I have no idea who you are. Why would you be worried about me? We don't know each other. Is this a joke?"

My stomach—and a few other organs—fell to my feet. How could he be so callous? I got humor. In fact, I loved joking around, but this was not the time. He knew I had disobeyed orders to save him, and we hadn't seen each other in two whole weeks. I didn't expect him to be so cavalier about my visit. I was hoping he would throw himself in my arms and go from there. Yes, I watched a lot of old movies. Even angels had hobbies.

"Stop messing around, Caleb, please. I was really worried. Gabriel—"

"Listen, dude. You seem like a nice guy, but I've never seen you before. You must have the wrong Caleb."

I was floored. He wasn't joking; he really couldn't remember me. *Hell and tarnation! That's what Gabriel meant by "taking care of things." He had Caleb's memory of me erased.* Short of killing him, of all the cruel things Gabriel could've done, this was probably the worst. To stand at that doorstep staring into the beautiful eyes of the one I couldn't take my mind off of and realize they didn't recognize me was pure hell. Angels don't have a murderous bone in their bodies—I believe we're simply incapable of it—but I also wanted to fly up to headquarters and kill Gabriel with my bare hands. The thought of my fingers wrapped around his neck like a vise was oddly pleasant, and yet also blood-curdling.

A small, soft voice reached my ears. "Don't be so fucking rude, Caleb." It was the young woman, looking up from her minute height into Caleb's eyes. "Will you invite him in for a cup of coffee already?"

Caleb's head snapped in her direction. "Watch that mouth of yours, girl. Don't let me hear you curse like a sailor again."

She rolled her eyes. "How would you know how sailors talk? If you dated once in a while, maybe you'd meet one or two."

"You are...." Obviously Caleb couldn't think of an appropriate comeback and turned his attention to me instead. "Right. Would you like to come in and maybe we can figure out how you think you know me?"

My heart had been crushed and I didn't know what to do. One thing I was certain of: I was not going to give up so easily. We had clicked once; we could do it again, right? I nodded, my tongue paralyzed by the knot in my throat, and followed the two into the house.

It was small with an interior that was both quaint and comfortable. The place was furnished with old furniture, likely salvaged from antique stores and flea markets. Not a single piece matched, and yet everything blended seamlessly like the edges of a watercolor painting, and just as beautiful. Yes, it suited Caleb, who in spite of his youth seemed to carry a much older soul inside, a certain strain on his broad shoulders, a slight heaviness to his step. I longed to know what caused that premature aging just as much as I yearned for the taste of his lips.

Caleb showed me to a small living room, and we sat across from one another, he on an armchair and I on the sofa. The elfin girl had left the room to fetch some coffee. I followed her with my eyes down the narrow corridor with curiosity. Who was she?

"That's my baby sister." Caleb read my mind, a smile on his face. "She's a pest but means well."

I laughed, a little more at ease and full of hope that he would remember me. "What's her name?"

The young woman answered the question as she entered the room carrying a small tray with a french press and some coffee cups. "My name's Joan. What's yours?"

I jumped to my feet to help her with the tray, but she waved me away. "I'm Sky."

The tray safely deposited on top of a small round table, Joan looked at me with a tiny, comical frown and inquisitive eyes. "Do you have a last name?"

I blushed. My last name was not one I volunteered very often. Not even to other angels. It was corny and so not me. "Heavensent. Sky Heavensent."

I half expected her to start laughing at my ridiculous name, but she bit her lower lip instead as if deep in thought. "I like it. It bodes well for us that Mr. Heavensent came knocking at our door."

A chuckle escaped my lips. I liked this young woman. She had spunk and was obviously very kind. Angels couldn't resist kindness. It was in our DNA, so to speak.

Caleb joined me, laughing softly. "Are you ever going to serve that coffee, girl?" Joan stuck her tongue out at him and poured a cup. "Joan makes the best coffee in town." I spied a little smile on her lips as she handed me the steaming cup. "And she's a great judge of character." She was smiling in earnest by that point, and I couldn't help but smile along.

Joan looked at me and winked. "In spite of being an old crank most of the time, my brother can be quite charming."

My breath caught in my throat watching Caleb's odd eyes light up at her words. There was such love there. I wanted to be the recipient of some of it and I couldn't be. Not anymore.

My eyes prickled and burned. "I shouldn't bother you any longer." My absence would be noticed if I stayed away too long, and as much as I didn't want to give up on Caleb, what good would lingering do, painfully realizing he didn't remember me any more than he remembered Gabriel? "I should go."

Caleb stood up. "No, please. Stay for dinner." It was just a polite invitation, I knew, but it still made my heart sing. I was tempted. Very tempted. *Can I get away with another hour or so?* "Something sent you to our door. I don't like to piss off fate."

Joan chimed in. "Yeah, he only likes pissing me off." She was rewarded with a swat from her brother's hand. "But he's right. Stay for dinner. I have pizza in the oven." Her voice took on a singsong tone, and I was inexplicably lulled into a sense of peace.

"Okay, I'll stay." I didn't even realize I was going to say it until the words were out of my mouth. But I did want to stay. As unwise as it may be, I needed this. "Very kind of you to ask."

I must've had a stupid smile on my face because Joan giggled. "Why so formal? You're not any older than my brother."

If only she knew how old I really was. I smiled at her, stealing a glance at Caleb, who seemed perfectly content sitting and watching his baby sister.

We ate around the small round table in the kitchen. Joan had a voracious appetite for someone so small, and I made a special effort not to eat more than one slice in case she needed more. Not that angels actually have to eat, but over the years I came to appreciate the flavor and pleasure of eating good human food. I was particularly partial to baked desserts. Since angels don't absorb calories, I could eat my weight in sugar and never put on a pound. Small perk of being an angelic creature.

While I was taking a gulp out of the gigantic glass of Coke Caleb had set in front of me, I noticed Joan watching me between bites, a funny expression on her face. "You do look terribly familiar," she said, a big chunk of pepperoni hanging from the corner of her mouth. "Not sure where I met you before, but I'm pretty sure I did."

That startled me. I was certain I had never met the little elf. "Don't think we've met." *I have met your brother though.* I bit my tongue so as not to let my thoughts out. "I just have that kind of face."

"What kind? The drop-dead-gorgeous kind that no one in their right mind would ever forget?" I choked on my drink, and I heard Caleb laugh. "Come on, guys, let's be serious. Mr. Heavensent here is a hottie. Ask him out, Caleb, won't you? If you don't, I just might."

My face and neck were taken by a growing burning heat. I coughed a little, avoiding Caleb's eyes.

"You're not old enough to date someone our age." It was Caleb's voice, still laughing under his breath. "You're barely eighteen, and Sky here is at least twenty-five."

"Then you do it." They seemed to have forgotten I was in the room, listening to every word. "God knows you haven't dated in ages. I don't need a fucking babysitter anymore. You can go out and enjoy your life now."

Caleb's eyes narrowed and he stopped laughing. "Young lady, I've warned you about the cursing." His voice had taken on a fatherly role, and I wondered where the real parents were. "I taught you better."

The young woman rolled her eyes again—*what's with teenagers and eye rolling?*—and crossed her arms in front of her. "All right then. I don't need a *freaking* babysitter anymore, and you can *freaking* date again. Is that better?"

From the corner of my eye, I noticed Caleb wasn't really angry at her. There was an amused little smile dancing in the corner of his lips. He didn't say anything for a few moments, as if pondering what to do next, but I expect he was only trying not to burst out laughing. "Who's up for some ice cream?"

Joan's eyes lit up like a child. "Yay! Sweetums?"

"Sure. Go get your coat." I had no idea what Sweetums was, but I was guessing it was an ice cream place. We were left alone in the room while the girl went to fetch a coat she really didn't need in the mild, end-of-summer evening. "You'll join us, right?" His voice, soft and sweet as honey, caressed my senses and a pleasant shiver ran through me. *Boy, Gabriel's wrath couldn't stop me!* "I'm glad you knocked at my door tonight. I haven't seen Joan so excited about anything in a while."

My heart fell. *Joan? Not you?*

"Are you coming or what?" Joan was already by the door, slipping her thin arms through the sleeves of a light jacket.

"We better go before she gets mad."

Caleb took a few steps toward me and closed his hand over my shoulder, prodding me in the direction of the door. An earthquake shook my whole being. If I were to guess, most likely an eight-point-five at least, with shock waves so strong it pushed my blood to the surface of my skin in a tidal wave of heat. He stopped suddenly as if he had felt it too, but it lasted only a few seconds. Maybe it was just my wishful thinking. "Let's go." *Is it my imagination or did his voice come out ever so slightly choked?*

Sweetums was just around the corner from their house, a happening place for the sleepy little town with people lining up outside the door. "You should try the lobster tracks flavor. It's awesome!" *Lobster in ice cream? Really?* Well, nobody could accuse me of not trying new things. I nodded with cautious enthusiasm, afraid of disappointing her if it turned out I didn't like it.

Caleb burst out laughing. "You should see your face, Sky. There is no lobster in lobster tracks ice cream. The lobster bits are just chocolate chunks tinted red to *look* like lobster."

Ah, that sounded a lot more appetizing. I loved the way Caleb's eyes crinkled at the corners when he laughed.

After getting our cones of generous servings of ice cream, we walked along the sidewalk, heading to the banks of Sheepscot River at a leisurely pace. We sat on a wooden bench by the pier and talked in hushed voices as if afraid to wake up the sleeping fauna. It felt right, as if we had been doing it for a long time. I suppose that was how it felt to have a family. To belong.

Too soon our ice cream was gone, and I had to once again face the fact that I must leave. Little Joan gave me a mighty hug and then sauntered away, blatantly leaving her brother alone with me. Caleb wiped his mouth with the back of his hand and stared at the ground as if searching for words. Did he feel the magnetic attraction from that beach two weeks before? Did he feel anything at all besides the awkwardness of being alone with someone his sister seemed hell-bent on matching him with?

I went first. "Thank you for a wonderful evening, Caleb. Your sister is awesome and—"

His hand shot out from his side and wrapped around mine. "Sorry I can't remember you, Sky." His eyes shone in the moonlight, and my skin prickled under his touch. "But it was an amazing evening. I would like to see you again." My heart quivered. "And so would Joan." He dropped his hand and I felt empty.

"I have a very tight schedule." It was true. I was also forbidden to leave Arcadia until further notice. "But I'll figure out a time to visit again. It'll be in the evening after work. Is that okay?"

I was so distracted by my need to pull him into my arms

that I almost flew. Catching myself right before my wings began unfurling, I waved goodbye to both of them, then jogged off the pier and away from them as quickly as my legs could carry me. My eyes burned with unshed tears, and my heart was about to burst. He didn't remember me at all.

***

DOLDRUMS

"No, no, no!" Cranky Amy's strident voice pierced my ears just as effectively as if she had stuck a needle in them. "Heavens above, Sky. You just can't seem to do anything right." I mumbled a stream of curses under my breath before looking up at her and smiling angelically. "And don't think that idiotic smile will work on me." She slammed a pile of folders on my desk and a big puff of old paper dust billowed into the air, making me cough. "Do these again. And do them right this time."

As she walked away, I fought the instinct to stick my tongue out at her. A bit childish maybe, but giving her the finger wasn't exactly proper for an angel. I stared at the pile of files she wanted me to go over again and sighed. I would've bet my life that she messed them up on purpose just to give me something boring to do. My memory was excellent and nowhere in it was the memory of me screwing up those old, musty files.

My eyes roamed to the window and the view of the Edge with longing. I wish I could be flying, pummeling down like an out-of-control aircraft, the wind shear making my body shake and my eyes burn. Instead, I was sitting at that desk shuffling through meaningless papers.

I focused ahead, as I was going to sneak down to Earth again to visit Caleb and his sister. The mere idea of seeing the one who filled my dreams and every waking thought made me happier than a puppy with a tennis ball. I had been visiting them almost every night for the past couple weeks, and those moments gave me a reason to endure the monotony of my days and look forward to my nights. Gabriel would have my feathers if he got wind of the time I was spending with the one he had so unfairly wiped of all memories of me. We were building new ones—or so I hoped.

My heart soared higher than my wings ever could when I spent time with Caleb. He still had absolutely no recollection of me but, however small, there was something growing between us. I lost my heart to him the first time I saw him, but I could feel—or maybe it was just wishful thinking—something tender developing between us.

I always fell too hard, too soon, and too deep in love. It was who I was. My mother used to say that I may have been born with a defective love gland, or maybe a hyperactive one considering other angels didn't seem to have that problem. I had fallen helplessly in love with Cloud, a tiny guardian angel who made the mistake of paying attention to me when I was still a fledgling. She had been so tired of my devotion that she quit the Guardians and joined an obscure corps with headquarters a few Heavens above mine and lived in absolute isolation. Later I attached myself, heart and soul, to a fierce angel of mercy who wasn't merciful enough to cut me off before I went in too deep. My heart seemed to have a very active imagination, if that were even possible. One smile, one kind word, and I was hooked.

With Caleb it felt very different though. Yes, I had once again fallen too fast and too deep for someone I barely knew, but instead of the typical anxiety-inducing pangs and yearnings, every time I laid eyes on him an overflowing sense of peace filled me.

So far we had gone out for lobster in the harbor, walked along the river at twilight, had coffee and warm bread at the local bakery, and hid in the sunken garden chuckling like little boys while Joan cursed her way through the streets of Wiscasset looking for us. Being with him was easy and carefree. Barring the fact that I kept my true identity secret from him, I could be myself around him. No pretenses, no games. Caleb seemed to enjoy my company in spite—or even because—of my quirkiness and penchant for blunder. With him, I could leave my 'liability' status and even my position in the Angelic Corps behind and be simply Sky.

"Are you finished yet?" Cranky Amy was back, her chubby cheeks puffed up in annoyance. The image of a puffer fish came to my mind and I laughed. She wasn't happy. "What are you laughing about? There's nothing funny about being lazy. You sit there all day, your mind a thousand miles away and with idle fingers."

The files were actually done. I wasn't the total nincompoop she made me out to be. The work may be boring, but it wasn't complicated. I handed the files to her with a smirk on my face.

"Are you sure these are done properly?" A little shiver of pleasure went through me at her look of disappointment. "Gabriel's going to flip if you messed them up again."

"They're done correctly." *As long as you don't mess them up again.* I held my tongue. Even though she was only an assistant, she had the ear of the archangel. And his trust. Amy worshiped the air Gabriel floated on and would do just about anything for him. He knew it and rewarded her with his trust. Their whole relationship reeked of nepotism and made me sick. "Gabriel will be pleased."

Reluctantly and with a little huff, she took the files and skittered away toward the stairs. I sighed and looked at my watch. It was almost time to leave. *If I play it right, I can start cleaning up right now and be done by the end of my shift.* I covertly looked around me and noticed I wasn't the only one with that idea; several other angels at nearby desks were already packing up their belongings, storing materials in drawers and cabinets.

My mind was racing way ahead of me. I would rush home, preen my wings a bit, and then as soon as the sunlight began to fade, I would fall off the Edge and fly down to what was quickly becoming my favorite place in the universe. I couldn't wait.

When the trumpets of the herald angels rang announcing the end of the workday, my heart was ready to burst with excitement. I jumped off my chair and ran to the door, forgetting all pretense of calm or decorum. Just as I was about to cross the threshold, I heard my name called.

It was Gabriel. *What could he possibly want?* I turned around slowly, careful not to show the irritation I was feeling inside. "Yes, Gabriel?"

He stood on the bottom step of the staircase, looking his usual sour self, his lips pursed and arms crossed over his chest. "I need you to run an errand for me."

"But Gabriel, it's time to go home." I probably sounded like a whiny child.

"You can do this on your way home." He stepped forward in my direction and handed me a piece of paper. "It's not like you have a social life anyway." True. I didn't. Not until Caleb. "I need you to stop at the flower shop and order a dozen seraphic roses to be delivered to this address by tomorrow afternoon. Make sure they are of the best quality."

Who's he trying to impress? Is he up for some kind of promotion and wants to woo whoever's in charge of hiring? A business prospect? I really didn't care, but it was annoying that he would delay me like that.

"Well, go! The shop will be closed in half an hour."

I wanted to ask him why he didn't do it himself, but I held my tongue. The shop was on my way home, and it would be just a few minutes extra. No point in getting on Gabriel's wrong side again. I took the paper and ran off.

The store was packed, of course. I waited in line for a good twenty minutes while the female angel in front of me took her sweet time deciding whether to order white lilacs or gardenias for her six-hundred-and-fiftieth birthday party. My thoughts were unworthy of an angel as I tapped my fingers on my arms, waiting for my chance to order. After what felt like an eternity, which said quite a lot for an angel, I was finally able to order the seraphic roses—"Purple or pink? I don't care, just make it quick"—and leave. Dusk was already staining the horizon and the Earth below me.

Anxious to get to Caleb's side and afraid that I may be too late, I flew even faster than my usual crazy speed and landed with a thump right behind their house. A cloud of dirt flew up into the air around me, and I spent the next five minutes dusting myself off.

Joan came to the door and hugged me as if she had known me her whole life. "Come on in. Maybe you can drill some sense into my unreasonable brother." *Uh-oh. What have I dropped into?*

Caleb was sitting at the kitchen table, pouring over what looked like bills, his reading glasses sliding down his nose and his teeth clamped over his upper lip. I licked my lips remembering how good his tasted and then, feeling guilty, moved my eyes away from Caleb's delicious mouth and to Joan's very angry eyes. The young woman was standing a couple feet away from me, arms crossed and her foot tapping angrily on the tiled floor.

"Can you tell my impossible brother that I have to go on this trip?" Joan said, surprising me off my thoughts. "My social life is hanging in the balance. If I don't go on this trip, I'll be forever marked as an outcast in my school."

Caleb looked up, noticing me for the first time, and smiled. "Don't be so dramatic. There are a lot of kids who aren't going." With his forefinger, he made a little circle in the air by his temple. "You'll survive. Trust me."

"I'll never be invited to any parties anymore, and my chances of meeting a suitable prom date will be destroyed." Joan didn't give up easily. I learned that very quickly.

"For God's sake, Joan. We can't afford it right now." Caleb sighed deeply and wiped a hand over his face. "I have too many bills to pay."

"What if I get a job? I hear Sweetums is hiring. What do you think, Sky? Shouldn't he stop being such an old cheapo and let me go?"

Stuck between a rock and a hard place, I blinked. What was I supposed to say? Conflict mediation was not my field of expertise. On one hand, I didn't want to displease Caleb, but I also didn't want to deal with Joan's wrath. She was young and tiny, but she could be fierce. "How much is it?" *Not what they were expecting to hear, I'm sure.*

"It'll cost only five hundred dollars and includes stay and food. It's dirt cheap."

I almost laughed; Joan sounded so convincing.

Caleb chuckled. "*Only* five hundred. I don't know what I was thinking. I know, I won't pay the electric bill. After all, we can go without heat and light for another month or so." The sarcasm in his voice was so thick I could almost see it.

Angels have money. It never occurred to me to ask where it came from, but the fact remained that we did have money available to us. We weren't paid a salary, but we used money to buy food and drinks, sometimes clothes and other things. When we were running out of money, we went to the Angelic Tender Machine—aka ATM—and withdrew whatever amount we needed, never more or less.

"Can I speak to you, Caleb?" Joan threw me a suspicious glance. "Alone?"

He took off his glasses and set them on the table before stepping into the living room with me. Joan was left in the kitchen, her eyes widening in either anger or hope—I wasn't quite sure which.

"I could pay for the trip." I braced myself for the explosion. In the short time I'd known him, I'd learned that Caleb was proud and unwilling to accept any handouts. He opened his mouth to protest, but I stopped him, raising my hand. "Hear me out first. I have some money put aside. It's just sitting there. I could lend it to you to be paid back whenever and however you can."

Eyes ablaze, Caleb smiled. "You're a good man, Sky. And a good friend." He took a step forward and laid a hand on my arm, sending millions of electric shocks through my body. "But you don't know Joan. She's a drama queen who'll go to extremes to get what she perceives to be of utmost importance only to blissfully forget about it a few days later."

From between shallow breaths I laughed. "The offer is there if you want it, but I understand if you don't." *Just keep your hand on my arm.* Much to my disappointment, he dropped his hand, leaving a pleasurable hot spot in its place.

"Thank you, Sky. I appreciate it." His unusual eyes

scanned me from head to toe, and blood rushed to my cheeks. *Holy mackerel!* With just a glance he'd set me on fire. "You look good." As soon as he said it, he laughed. "Sorry. That sounded pretty cheesy." I didn't care. I was a cheesy angel. I smiled, willing him to compliment me again, but he moved on. "Let's ignore my sister for as long as we can bear it and then decide what to do about the damned field trip."

We did. For the rest of the evening, we were confronted with Joan's evil eye and scowling. At one point during our dinner at the local burger joint, I imagined her with an eye patch and a parrot on her shoulder. Heavens knew she wouldn't stop grumbling like a pirate in pain. Caleb and I pretended we didn't notice and enjoyed our evening together.

"Come on, Joan, be a grown-up for once and stop acting like a spoiled two-year-old," Caleb finally said, tired of her frown and icy attitude. "What about that ice cream you love so much?"

Joan's face relaxed ever so slightly at the mention of the treat, and I jumped on it. "I'll buy you the biggest cone they sell. What do you say?"

She gave me a half-hearted scowl and then nodded. It was the waving of a white flag. I ran into the store and made good on my promise.

The two siblings stayed outside in the chilly evening, sitting on a bench across the street. When I left Sweetums, balancing a gargantuan ice cream cone in my hand, I looked up to where they were waiting and caught Caleb watching me. I almost dropped the cone. There was heat in that look and something else—tenderness and yearning. My heart skipped a few beats and I stumbled a little.

"I thought you were going to drop my ice cream." Joan made a dash for the cone and yanked it from my hand. "What were you thinking?"

My lips stretched into a smile as I raised my eyes to Caleb's. "I had my mind on lavender fields. Beautiful, never-ending fields."

Caleb bit his lower lip, and I watched in idiotic fascination as his Adam's apple bobbed up and down. Oh yes, I had fallen hard!

***

THE CALL

Filing mission papers had to be by far the most tedious job ever invented. After the first two hours of my shift, I was ready to poke my eyes out or volunteer for the cemetery squad—the crew in charge of accounting for each soul taken by the "other side." Not a job any of us aspired to. Having to witness that kind of agony on a regular basis could drive even the most stable of angels to madness.

Another week had passed since I'd seen Caleb, and time dragged by as if wearing lead-lined boots. Gabriel still showed no sign of forgiveness, which was pretty ironic considering who he was. He was taking great pleasure in assigning me to the dreariest of tasks. For an angel, he was proving to be particularly twisted.

"Gabriel wants you to go to central storage to look for file 10235B," Amy yelled from the other side of the room. Everybody else was out on mission, leaving no doubt the order was aimed at me. The job would get me moving at least—I couldn't even feel my feet anymore.

Central storage was on the other side of headquarters and a nice walk along the Edge of Arcadia, an area where you could look down at the Earth below. The land of the mortals was a beauty, and I could never get enough of staring at it. With its amazing green forests, immense blue oceans, and never-ending brownish deserts, the human Earth was an amazing piece of art. To me, nothing in the angelic world even compared to it. I strolled along the Edge, drooling and dreaming. Caleb was down there, not remembering me and by now probably forgetting our short meeting the week before.

With a sigh, I entered the ugly, square building that sheltered all the files from past soul collections and headed for the main room where I could scroll the database for the file's location. I found it quickly and headed for the upper floors, where the microchip with the file was located, but stopped midway. A thought came to me. *Are Caleb's parents dead? Is that why he seems to be a mixture of brother and father to young Joan?* I spun on my heels and went back to the computer to look for their names. All I had to go by was their last name and their progeny, which made it a little more complicated, but if there was something I'd learned to do in the many times I'd been relegated to my desk job, it was research. I was, in fact, very good at it.

It took me about ten minutes, but I found it: Elaine and Malcolm Pierce, parents of Caleb and Joan Pierce, souls collected almost ten years back from the wreck of a car accident. Ten years…. Caleb would've been around eighteen and Joan around eight. My heart went out to them. Both orphaned at an early age. No wonder Caleb carried that subtle weight on his shoulders, the weight of responsibilities thrown at him prematurely. The weight of youth cut short.

I jotted down the location of the file and, throwing caution to the wind, I unfurled and flapped my wings up to the upper floors instead of using the stairs. Let them see me disobeying orders in the surveillance camera. What could they do to me that they hadn't done already?

The original file I was sent for was pretty easy to find since it was about a much more recent death, but it took me a long while to find Caleb's parents'. It was almost as if Gabriel didn't want anyone to find it. I realized that was exactly what had happened. Gabriel didn't want anyone to know the true nature of my screwup, so he was hiding anything connected to Caleb. Carefully, I removed the chip from its receptacle and slipped it into the pocket of my jeans. As it turned out, Gabriel's overcautious move had given me the chance to peruse the file at home without the fear of someone noticing it was gone.

Amy was at the door to the office, a purplish tint to her round cherubic face and her arms wrapped tightly across her chest. I was hit in the face by the heat of her anger. "Two hours? Really? It took you two full hours to fetch a tiny little file?" Her voice came out more growl than words. "You are by far the most incompetent angel I have ever met."

Even though it wasn't uncommon for me to be the target of similar comments, it still bothered me. I wasn't *that* incompetent, was I? I definitely marched to the beat of a different drum, but did that make me incompetent? I scowled at her in response and handed her the chip. "Have you been to that place lately? It's huge and these files are tiny." The excuse sounded ridiculous even to my own ears, but I couldn't let it go.

I spun on my feet and trotted to my desk, where I was planning to sulk thoroughly and fully for the next few hours. But as soon as I sat down, my phone vibrated in my pocket. My heart skipped a beat. I never got calls on that phone—the advantages or disadvantages of not having many friends, you decide—and when I did, it was normally bad news of some kind. Gabriel called me on that number when I totally ignored him on the official seraphic phone, a dinosaur of a contraption that would make any tech-savvy person cringe.

I didn't recognize the number on the caller ID at first, but then it hit me—it was Joan's number. *Why is she calling me?*

"Sky?" Her voice came through high-pitched and hysterical. Something was wrong. "It's Caleb. He's in the hospital."

My stomach followed my heart in its funny hopscotch race. "What do you mean he's in the hospital? What happened?"

I felt rather than heard her sobs and her tears of panic. "He was in a terrible accident. I didn't know who to call. We have no family and Caleb has no friends. Not anyone I could call for something like this."

"Calm down." The words were more for me than her. My heart was racing a thousand miles a second, and I could taste bile. *Was this Gabriel? He promised he wouldn't hurt him.* "Where are you?"

"I'm at the hospital. Can you come?" The request was made in a tiny voice as if she were scared I would turn her down.

I was going to get in all kinds of trouble. "Which hospital? I'll be there as soon as I can."

I barely hit the disconnect button before I was out the door, running toward the Edge. I could hear Amy's exasperated voice yelling behind me, but I was beyond caring. Caleb was hurt. The one thing that really mattered to me was in danger.

I managed to alight in a deserted and sheltered alley behind the hospital. Surveying the grounds, I furled my wings and walked around the corner to the front. I was well-acquainted with this hospital. In fact, I was very familiar with all the hospitals in the area because of my job. But this was a different situation. I wasn't here to harvest a soul but to make sure I didn't have to. Again.

As I crossed the swinging doors of the ER, I spied Joan's small figure curled up on a chair, her head against her knees.

"Joan," I said softly, trying not to call too much attention to myself. An angel, even in his human form, can't help but attract attention. The good thing about hospitals was that people were always too busy either saving lives or worrying about them to pay much attention to their surroundings. That made my undercover job much easier.

Joan's head popped up at the sound of my voice, and she propelled herself off the chair and into my arms. "So glad you're here, Sky." Her mouth was crushed into the middle of my chest, but I could still hear the sobbing. "I don't know what I'll do if I lose him."

You and me both, girl.

I caressed the top of her head and gently prodded her toward a less crowded corner of the waiting room. We sat side by side on the small blue seats, her head still cradled in my hand, resting on my shoulder. "Calm down. You're not going to help him by freaking out." *Hypocrite*. My anxieties were through the roof, and if I didn't have to comfort the elfin girl, I would be unwisely stomping through the hallways of the hospital trying to find Caleb. "Tell me what happened."

She took a couple deep breaths, bracing herself to talk. "I don't understand how this happened." Hiccups punctuated her speech. "Ever since his motorcycle accident a few weeks ago, he hasn't driven anywhere. He's been waiting for the insurance to pay for a new bike. But someone called and told him his bike was ready for pickup."

I frowned. "The insurance?"

"That's what we figured. They didn't identify themselves." Joan pulled a tissue out of her pocket and blew her nose. "They gave him the address and he left. I wanted to go with him, but he insisted I needed to work on this paper for school and that he would be back soon." The hiccups turned to sobs again. "The next thing I know, I get a call from the hospital telling me he was in a terrible bike accident." She was bawling, and I wanted to do the same.

The whole thing smelled like a rat. An angelic rat. "What exactly happened?"

She raised her eyes to mine. Joan was pretty, but she didn't have her brother's beautifully multicolored eyes. "The thing is, Sky, there's no way he could've picked up the bike from the shop, got on it, and had an accident. I got that call not even fifteen minutes after he left. It would've taken him at least half an hour—probably more—to get there."

Definitely angelic rat stench. "Where is Caleb now?"

"In surgery." Her eyes filled with tears anew. Where was Caleb's guardian angel? I bet Caleb had been removed from the list since he was supposed to have died three weeks ago. "I can't lose him, Sky. I just can't." Her eyes latched on to mine, a hint of a request reflected among the desperation. "You can do something about it, can't you?" It was a mere whisper, but it shook me to the bone.

I swallowed. Hard. "What do you mean by that?"

"You're an angel. You can help him."

If I hadn't been sitting, I would've fallen on my butt. How did she know that?

"Don't be silly. How can I be an angel? Angels don't exist." As proficient as I was at telling lies—for an angel, anyway—this one was hard to utter out loud.

"I knew it as soon as I opened the door the night you came looking for Caleb," she continued, her eyes never leaving mine. My mouth dropped open, but no sound came out. "I've seen an angel before." Her statement echoed Caleb's words to me that first time we met.

"When?" I didn't even bother to disguise my surprise.

"The night of our accident." Her hand tightened over mine as if she needed to anchor herself to something. "After the car skidded and ran over the cliff, one of you came to get my parents' souls. I was barely conscious, but I remember it well. Something about your eyes is like that angel's. When I tried to grab his hand, he told me it wasn't my time yet and that I would be all right."

Caleb must have seen it too. I didn't know they'd been with their parents at the time of their deaths. I didn't know what to say. *Should I lie? Or should I just go along with it?*

"You can help him, right?" Her voice was pleading, desperate.

Unfortunately, I didn't have any special healing powers. I was only a collector, not a giver. I hung my head, disgusted with myself. What was the use of being an angel if I couldn't even save the one I loved? "I'm an angel of death, Joan," I told her in a hushed voice. "I take. I can't give back."

Her brown eyes widened in horror. "You're not going to take him, are you?" She moved a few inches away from me as if my proximity hurt her.

"No, no, of course not." I couldn't tell her I loved him, could I? And I definitely couldn't tell her that Caleb should already be dead. "I just can't help much, that's all. We'll have to hope the doctors do their magic. I'm sorry, Joan. I really, really am sorry."

Time trickled by; the only way I knew how long it had been was by the fact that it was dark outside. We sat together, her head on my shoulder, my head on hers. I wondered what people thought, seeing the two of us like that. Physically, we couldn't be any more different. Joan was like Caleb in many ways: she had dark, almost black hair and a smooth, light tan that contrasted heavily with my angel-white skin. Caleb was very tall, unlike his sister who couldn't be much taller than five feet, but they were both slim and had well-defined lips. The biggest difference was the eyes. Where his were that unusual combination of green and violet, hers were honeyed brown.

My phone vibrated in my pocket and I jumped, startled. "Shit! It's Gabriel!" Joan blinked at me, uncomprehending. I put a finger in front of my lips. "Shhh, don't say a word. It's my boss."

"Angels have bosses?" She must've been asleep, for her eyes looked unfocused and bleary.

I raised my finger to my lips again and pressed Talk. "Gabriel?"

Needless to say he wasn't happy, but then again, when was the last time Gabriel had even smiled? "Are you totally out of your mind?" I hoped the other people in the waiting room couldn't hear the archangel's irate voice. "What makes you think it's okay to leave work in the middle of the day like that?" I exhaled in relief. He didn't know where I was. "Without as much as a simple request. What in Heaven's name is your problem?"

I took a long breath and braced myself to be deceptive

once again. Every time I lied, a little piece of my angel soul seemed to break away. "I wasn't feeling well, and Amy was being very unreasonable." It wasn't a total lie. "I've done everything you've asked of me. I need a day off to clear my head. Please, Gabriel."

On the other end of the line I could hear Gabriel whisper in Seraphic, a quirk of his when he was collecting his thoughts. "All right then. I'm feeling generous today." Like hell he was. "You can take the rest of the day off, but you better be at work on time tomorrow."

I raised my eyes upward and said a silent prayer of thanks to the big boss. Not sure he had anything to do with it, but I liked to think he was all merciful and not too attached to rules and regulations like Gabriel and the other archangels were. I heard the telltale click of the call being disconnected and put the phone away.

Joan was staring at me as if I were a two-headed alien—which I guess I kind of was. "Gabriel? As in Archangel Gabriel?"

I nodded, scanning the room to make sure no one was listening. "Yes, but please keep your voice down." My whisper sounded too loud to my nervous ears. "No mortal is supposed to know we really exist."

Forgetting her woes for a moment, she giggled. "Yeah, like I want to start telling people I'm friends with an actual angel. That would make me really popular." Her smile died quickly and was replaced by a grimace. "Why did you say you were worried about Caleb?"

I slid my hand down my face. What could I say? "Long

story for another day." Dodging the answer was better than lying, and I didn't feel she—or I—was ready for the truth yet. What would she think of me if I told her how her brother and I had met?

A doctor in scrubs came through the heavy gray doors, removing his surgical mask. "Miss Pierce," he called, scanning the room. We both jumped to our feet in unison and rushed to the man who looked at me in confusion. "You are?"

Joan stepped forward, ignoring his question. "My brother, how's he doing?" Her voice quivered and I placed my hands on her shoulders to steady her.

The doctor, still eyeing me suspiciously, seemed too exhausted to question my presence. "He's out of surgery now."

Joan's shoulders tensed under my hands. "And how did it go? How serious is it?" A gurgling sound came from her mouth and her whole body shook. "Is he going to make it?"

"Yes." Never had such a tiny word made me so happy and relieved. "He's not out of the woods yet though. He suffered a traumatic brain injury. We're hoping the surgery fixed it, but as is often the case with these kinds of injuries, only time will tell if there are any lingering problems."

Caleb's little sister leaned against me, slumping from relief or worry, not sure which. "When can I see him?" I'd never had the chance to comfort someone like that. Not while still alive. It felt good.

"He'll most likely be unconscious for a long while," the doctor said. "You may want to go home and rest."

"No!" She was so emphatic the doctor seemed genuinely surprised. "I want to be with him when he wakes up. Can I be in his room? Please?"

I stepped in. "Surely you can let her curl up on a chair in his room. He's the only family she has."

In the end, the doctor arranged for a recliner to be moved to Caleb's ICU room so she could sleep there. I wasn't allowed to see him since I wasn't family so, as hard as it was for me to leave Joan alone in the hospital, I had to get back to Arcadia before my boss figured out what I was up to. Before I left, Joan wrapped her arms around my middle so tight I was afraid she wouldn't let me go.

I was already on my way up, hidden by the dark of the night, when I felt a tug. Not in the physical sense, but as if someone were reaching out to my thoughts, which was ridiculous. Angels didn't have the power of telepathy—at least not us poor schmucks on the bottom of the seraphic hierarchy. But there it was, clear as day and just as strongly as real fingers reaching into my thoughts. I stopped midair and, without much hesitation, I turned back. Silently I hovered over the hospital, considering the pros and cons of what I was about to do. Decision made, I did the only true magical thing I knew: made myself invisible so I could enter the hospital unseen. I wasn't really invisible, but I could manipulate people's perceptions so they would see nothing other than wavering air. I entered the hospital and, with a sense of urgency growing in my heart, flew to the only room I cared about.

Joan was already curled up on the chair, fast asleep under

the white hospital blanket. When I turned my attention to the bed, my heart came suddenly alive, thumping so loud and hard I was afraid someone would hear it. Caleb looked peaceful in spite of all the wires going to and from him. His head was wrapped in bandages, and his beautiful face was scratched and bloody. His left arm was also heavily bandaged and propped on a cushion. I stepped closer to the bed and sat on the edge, my eyes incapable of moving away from the sleeping figure of the man I loved. My heart was so full I thought it would burst. My unfurled wings came around me to create a feathery shelter over my love, and I finally allowed the tears that burned in my eyes to run free.

I didn't know love could be this painful.

WAKING UP
LONELY HEARTS

Angels don't have siblings. Not sure why that is, considering we do have parents. I must say that having Joan in my life felt good in spite of the circumstances. As independent and capable as she obviously was, she needed a shoulder to lean on in her hour of need. And my shoulder was very willing. Not just because she was Caleb's sister, but because it felt good to have someone who actually needed me and trusted me to do the right thing.

Unfortunately, I had Gabriel to deal with, and he wasn't an easy one to fool. My daily escapades to be by Caleb's side were getting harder and harder to accomplish and, since stealth had never been my strong angelic feature, also very hard to hide from others. Sooner or later I was bound to get caught. *Will I be the first angel ever to go to prison? Since there are no real prisons in Arcadia, they'll have to build one just for me....* My thoughts wandered into the usual weird places my imagination always seemed to carry me.

It was late, nearly time for the end of my shift. I looked

around and was happy to see everyone had left. Even Cranky Amy, who always lingered until everyone else had gone home. Gabriel was probably still lurking around as he always did—did he not have a life outside these walls? It was my chance to leave unnoticed.

The fact that Caleb was still unconscious worried me at first, but the doctors explained it was an induced sleep to give his brain time to restore and heal. In the back of my mind, I had this crazy dream that Caleb would wake up and remember our first encounter weeks before. Even angels can dream!

I tiptoed my way to the door, opening it slowly and quietly.

"Where do you think you're going?" Gabriel's booming voice startled me.

The door handle slid from my hand and the heavy door slammed shut, the resulting bang echoing throughout the room. *So much for a quiet exit.*

"I'm going home." The only plausible lie I could come up with at the time. He knew I had no friends, and there wasn't much for a lonely angel like me to do in town.

"There are still ten minutes left in your shift." He was right. Petty but right. "I need you to make a phone call for me because I have to leave a little earlier today." He was all dressed up and was carrying a small bunch of flowers. *Does he have a date? Who in their right mind would date him?* "Go to my office and find the number for Archangel Michael in my Rolodex."

I rolled my eyes; I couldn't help it. A Rolodex? Was he

still living in the dark ages?

He frowned but continued. "Call him and tell him I'll be a few minutes late for our meeting tomorrow because I must interview new angels for the squad."

Waiting for further instructions, I stared at him. I was still wondering who he could possibly be dating.

He gave me "the look." The one that could melt rocks. I snapped to it. "Sure, Gabriel, right away."

With him gone, I ran up the stairs to his office and entered the gauzy-walled room. It was easy to see that Gabriel was a soldier by training. Everything in his space had a purpose, and nothing was out of place; I knew to leave it all the same way I found it. His Rolodex was massive, containing more numbers and addresses than I had ever seen, but finding Michael's was easy—he had bookmarked it with a paperclip. I sat on his extremely comfortable chair and unwisely propped my feet on top of his desk while I dialed the number and waited for someone to pick up.

"Archangel Michael's office. How may I help you?" The squeaky voice of Michael's secretary, Ariel, had always grated on my nerves. Ariel was a big guy with strong, wide shoulders and a lot of muscle, but somehow none of that strength had reached his vocal cords. He sounded like Donald Duck on helium.

Quickly I gave him the message and hung up before he had the chance to scratch my eardrums with his voice again. I allowed myself a few more seconds in Gabriel's chair as I scanned the top of the desk.

A notepad caught my eye. The top page was scribbled

on in big fancy letters, but what really made me look twice was the language of the note. It was in Seraphic. I had heard Gabriel speak in Seraphic a lot lately, and to find a written note in that language raised my alarms. I had been to Gabriel's office more times than I cared to admit, and never once had I seen a Seraphic note. He was trying to hide something.

Swinging my legs off the desk, I pulled my phone out of my pocket and took a picture of the note. I had to find out what it said. Maybe I was being paranoid, but it seemed strange that Gabriel's sudden fondness for a dead language surfaced at the same time as Caleb's fiasco. I slid the phone back into my pocket and left headquarters, crossing paths with Cranky Amy on my way out. I waved at her and pressed on, afraid she would find something else for me to do.

Never one to be too concerned about the way I dressed, oddly enough I took great pains to look halfway attractive—or what I thought was attractive in the realm of the mortals—every time I went to visit Caleb. It wasn't as if he could see me anyway, but I felt the need to look good in his eyes, even if those mesmerizing eyes were closed. I put on a fresh pair of jeans and a plain black T-shirt that hugged my chest. Another perk of being an angel was having a well-toned body without having to lift as much as a bag of potatoes.

Recently, while I was at the hospital watching TV shows and eating chips with Joan, I had been informed by the elfin girl that hard pecs and abs were in great demand in the human world. "You would kill in a bathing suit," she'd said. I wasn't certain "killing" anything was a good thing, but she seemed to think it was. I was beginning to have a great deal of respect for her opinion, so the muscle-hugging T-shirt was probably a good choice for the occasion.

Since Gabriel seemed to have gone on a date, I was a little more at ease leaving again. Still, I decided to err on the side of caution and made sure no one was watching when I unfurled my white wings, silvery under the moonlight, and jumped off the Edge, plummeting to my beloved Earth below. The air rushing against my skin made my eyes water and my heart leap in excitement. *When will I be able to do this all day?* If it were up to my incredibly unfair boss, most likely never again.

They couldn't land an angel forever, could they?

Joan ran to me as soon as she saw me. "You're late." Her words were more of a statement than an accusation. She hugged me so tight I whimpered a little, unused as I was to shows of affection. A few seconds later, she grabbed my hand and forcibly pulled me in the direction of Caleb's ward. "Come quick. The doctors are going to take him off the sedative."

I stopped abruptly, and she bounced back like a rubber band and slammed into me. Caleb was going to wake up. Would he remember me? Would he remember anything at all? The doctors warned that it was possible he would suffer from temporary amnesia due to his brain injury. I was scared all of a sudden. What if he couldn't even remember me from my visit to his house?

"What?" Joan seemed perplexed by my hesitation. "We want to be there when he wakes up." *Not sure I do.* "What are you afraid of?" She pulled on my hand again. "Let's go."

In spite of my doubts, I did want to see those eyes again. I followed her into the ICU and his room. Nothing seemed to have changed since my visit the night before. He was still heavily bandaged and attached to all kinds of wires that snaked into many different beeping machines. But even from underneath all that surgical paraphernalia, Caleb was gorgeous. The dark stubble that normally covered his face and chin had grown thicker. I longed to touch it and stuffed my hands in my pockets to keep from doing so, moving my eyes from his face to my feet.

"You are so screwed." Her voice was hushed, but I could still hear the amusement.

My eyebrow shot up in question. "What are you talking about, girl?"

"You're in love with my brother, aren't you?" My cheeks went from cool to tropical hot in a wink. How did she know that? "Get off it already! It's so obvious. The way you look at him makes me feel like a peeping tom."

I thought of denying it, but to what end? Might as well admit it and move on. "Yes, I'm very much in love with Caleb. But you can't tell him that, and this is not the right time to discuss it."

She squinted. "Why not? He's single, and God knows he could use a little loving in his life." Joan smiled, throwing a loving glance at her sleeping brother. "He's done nothing but take care of me since our parents died. He has no life of his own, and it's about time he gets one."

We sat on the chairs by the bed, Joan half turned to me,

her right leg curled under her. "He had just turned eighteen when it happened, and he took it upon himself to be the mom and dad I lost. I was a little kid, not even eight yet." I stole a glance toward the unmoving figure on the bed. "But now I'm all grown up and I feel guilty that he's so lonely. He barely has any friends, never dates, never goes out unless it's with me. He needs a life."

My thoughts exactly. Why couldn't Gabriel see it that way?

"What makes you think he would even be interested in me?" I had to ask. Even as an angel I had noticed that humans were a little peculiar when it came to same-sex relationships. As if hearts could choose whom they loved.

"My brother may not date much at all, but he's never kept his homosexuality from me—or from anyone else, for that matter." She bit her index fingernail, tears dancing in her eyes. "I just want him to be happy. He deserves it."

I pulled her hand from her mouth and held it in mine. "I do too." I did. Even though I wanted him to remember me and love me like my lonely heart loved him, I wanted him to be happy. Even if that didn't include me.

The hours ticked away and Joan's eyes began to close. I pulled our chairs closer together and cradled her head against me so she could rest for a while. I didn't need a lot of sleep—another perk of angelic life—and I selfishly wanted to be the first face Caleb saw when he woke up. So I stubbornly kept my eyes open and trained on Caleb as his sister snored gently against my shirt. I stroked her hair, my heart feeling both content and scared.

In the wee hours of the morning, my relentless eyes noticed a tiny twitch in Caleb's lips, shortly followed by an almost imperceptible movement of his eyes. My heart leaped, and I had to fight the urge to jump up from the chair and throw myself across the small space between me and the bed. Caleb was waking up! And just like joy had jump-started my heart a few seconds before, now fear grasped me solidly in its cruel fist.

***

COMING TO

One thing no one could accuse me of was being a scaredy-cat. On the contrary, I had often been called reckless and impulsive. Not because I was particularly brave or daredevilish, but because my brain—and more often than not, my heart—didn't ever allow me much time to think before I acted. When Caleb began moving, I was paralyzed by fear, a very unfamiliar feeling for me. All these questions and scenarios ran through my hyperactive brain.

What if he doesn't recognize me? Stupid! He already doesn't know who you are. What if he can't stand the sight of you? What if he has brain damage and can't remember anything at all? Shut up, brain!

I was at least well acquainted with my crazy internal monologues. When you lead the life of a lonely angel, branded as the weird one by all the other angels, you start going a little mad. Loneliness does that to you. One day you realize you're having whole conversations with yourself. Who else would you talk to after all?

The fear tightened my throat like a vise and wouldn't let me go. My heart was beating so fast it was a good thing I was an angel and couldn't suffer coronaries.

Joan stirred against my chest and pulled me out of my fear-induced stupor.

"He's waking up." She jumped off the chair, leaving my arms feeling empty. Perched on the edge of the bed, close to her brother's head, Joan laughed softly. "Caleb, can you hear me?"

Not sure my legs would hold me, much less carry me, I stood up, divided between unfurling my wings and fleeing and staying for the big reveal. I was better at dealing with the dead than the living. Nevertheless, I slowly approached the bed and stood behind Joan, where I could watch Caleb stir back to the land of the living.

"Caleb, can you hear me?" Joan had intertwined her fingers with her brother's and was cooing like a turtle dove. "Come on, bro, say something. I miss you."

I miss you too.

As if on cue, Caleb's eyes opened and the sight of that lavender-green combination almost blasted me off my feet. He blinked a few times before directing his focus at his sister's face leaning over him, desperate for a sign of recognition. His lips slowly stretched into a smile. "Joan." His voice was barely audible. "Sis."

Incapable of controlling it anymore, Joan practically threw herself across his body. "Oh my God, you fool. You scared me half to death." I heard her crying and laughing at the same time, her face buried in her brother's neck. "What the hell were you thinking driving that stupid bike?"

Celeb's muffled voice uttered something unintelligible.

"What did he say?" I asked, straining to see Caleb from behind Joan.

She straightened herself and looked up at me, her eyes a little haunted. "He said he wasn't on a bike."

I was floored. The rat smell was getting stronger. The EMTs and hospital personnel all said his injuries were consistent with those caused by a motorcycle accident. I agreed, for I had harvested many souls from the metal wreckage of bikes.

Forgetting my fear that he wouldn't remember me, I leaned over the bed beside Joan. "What happened, Caleb? What happened to you?" A terrible suspicion invaded my thoughts and I couldn't shake it. "Can you tell me?"

His eyes wandered to mine and rested there. A wave of warmth washed over me and my anxiety melted away. "Sky?" His hoarse voice sounded like a melody to my ears. He remembered me! "What are you doing here?"

Joan didn't let me answer. "He's been taking care of me while you were sleeping." She cupped his bruised cheek with one hand. "Because you got on that bike and nearly killed yourself. Again!"

I sat on the edge of the bed, my hand itching to hold Caleb's. "You said you weren't on the bike. What did you mean by that?"

Caleb licked his cracked lips and blinked a few times. "It's all very confusing." His eyes bounced from me to his sister. "I was on my way to pick up the bike." He had to stop and catch his breath. "One minute I was getting off the bus, the next I was on a bike speeding down the avenue and heading into incoming traffic. I don't understand…."

"Have you ever had blackouts before?" I asked, a funny feeling in my gut. There it was, the stench of a dead rat again.

Joan's head snapped up to look at me. "No, he never had any such thing." A quick glance at Caleb confirmed she was telling the truth. It wasn't a blackout. *What's going on?*

After a moment's hesitation, I decided it wasn't the right time to analyze a situation I was beginning to suspect had something to do with angelic intervention. "Never mind that now, Caleb. You need to rest and get better first."

There was a little smile on Caleb's lips. "Can I get some water?"

Joan jumped to her feet and was out the door in search of water before I could even offer to do it for her.

I was left alone in the room with the man I so desperately loved. Yes, it sounded ridiculous to be so infatuated with someone I barely knew, but angels tended to feel everything to the extreme. Just like the speed of my wings, I had gone from attracted to head over heels in love with this soul I had been sent to harvest. Almost fearfully, I edged closer to him, my hand on the blanket mere inches from his.

"Do you remember me?" I had to know. He'd called me

by my name earlier, but what did that really mean?

Caleb's eyebrow lifted in a deep arch. "Of course." My heart skipped a beat. "You had dinner with us a little while ago. You thought you had met be before." And just as quickly my heart plummeted. Not what I was hoping to hear. "Did you think I lost my memory?"

I smiled sadly. "No, though I wanted to make sure." It was not a lie. "I'm glad you remember."

To my great surprise and delight, he suddenly grabbed my hand. "Thank you," he whispered, his beautiful eyes shiny and tender. "For taking care of Joan while I was here."

"I didn't really take care of her," I protested softly. "She's perfectly capable. We kept each other company. She helped me as much as I helped her." *Isn't that the truth?*

He squeezed my hand. "Thank you. I owe you big time."

Another sad smile crept to my lips as I wondered whether I had made things worse by saving him the first time. This last accident didn't seem… natural. Something was off, and I was going to find out what. Unconsciously, I rubbed the side of his hand with my thumb, thrilled at how that simple touch could ignite such heat in me. Caleb didn't flinch, allowing me the small caress, his eyes never leaving mine.

"Can't leave you alone." Joan was standing by the door, staring at us and smiling. "A hospital isn't exactly the place for romance, you know. You should be ashamed of yourselves."

My face and neck burned so I let go of his hand. Caleb chuckled. "Brat!"

"Asshole." In a few quick steps, she crossed the space to

the bed and hugged her brother. "But I love you."

Caleb was still laughing, the sound muffled by Joan's body. "You're going to suffocate me." It was a weak protest, but she let him go all the same. Caleb looked at me, a smile still lighting his bruised face. "You'll get used to her. She's an acquired taste."

She smiled over at me. "But once you get used to me, you'll never be able to let me go."

I knew that. I was already hooked. For whatever reason, I was emotionally attached to this elfin girl. I felt protective and comfortable around her. *Is this what it feels like to have a sibling?*

"Like a rash you can't get rid of." The statement earned Caleb a pointed look from his sister, who I was sure would've punched him were he not injured in a hospital bed.

With much regret, I realized the night was practically over and soon the sun would be up. I had to return to Arcadia before anyone missed me. Saying goodbye was never easy, but for some reason that time was harder. I held Joan in a hug, my heart heavy with apprehension. If my suspicions were right, Caleb could be in a lot of danger, and I wasn't sure how I could change that.

Before I left, I turned one last time to look at Caleb. His eyes were closed again and his breathing had slowed. A sigh escaped my lips.

"He'll be okay," I heard Joan whisper behind me. "You'll be okay."

I smiled, waved, and left my heart behind.

SAMAEL
POISON

Not even the beautiful sight from the Edge could distract me. It was the third time I'd walked by, looking but not seeing, too preoccupied with whatever kind of dark forces were at play or who was pulling the strings of Caleb's fragile life. I was certain the hand of some seraphic force had something to do with his accident. Gabriel had promised he wouldn't hurt Caleb, but there were others who wouldn't have any qualms about taking the life of one who was already supposed to be dead.

I was due back at my desk in less than ten minutes, my lunch break almost over. I was queasy, a strange feeling for an angel. *Maybe I should talk to Gabriel. Ask him about what's happening.* No, I couldn't do that. Then I'd have to admit to breaking the rules and flying down to Earth, seeing the one I saved, getting involved in things an angel shouldn't get mixed up in. I'd have to find out some other way.

With my hands stuffed in the pockets of my jeans, I made myself go back to headquarters, my eyes on the ground, my back hunched. *Is love always this complicated? This painful?* I sat at my desk and slumped over the top, eyeing the tower of files and useless papers Amy had piled on it. What was the use? What good was I doing with the work given to me? Why wasn't I out there doing something worthy of an angel? Or even worthy of a human being? I rested my forehead on the desk and sighed loudly.

"Romantic woes, Sky?" Amy's annoying, high-pitched voice grated in my ears. "Angels and love don't mix. You should've learned that a long time ago."

What a crock of shit! Angels and love don't mix? Whatever happened to the concept that angels *were* love? That our main goal and mission was to spread love and protect it? Even my job as a death angel was supposed to be an act of love, bringing the freshly departed ones to their ultimate destination, a place of love and warmth. Where had things gone so wrong that angels were now condemning the act of love? The very emotion they had been created to protect and serve?

I bit my tongue, fully aware that if I told her exactly what I thought of her comment, I'd be in even bigger trouble.

Stewing in irritation, I rummaged through my pockets for heavenly money, wanting to get a cup of coffee in the vending machine. Buried deep within my pocket was my phone. I pulled it out and punched in the password. A picture appeared on the screen, the one I had taken of the note on Gabriel's desk. I had forgotten about it, but now my curiosity was awake. There was a Seraphic translator in the community room. The problem was I had no reason to go there now that my lunch hour was over.

I jumped out of my chair like a metal coil and propelled myself toward the stairs. *Think this through, Sky. Think this through.* I climbed the stairs two and three steps at a time and found myself facing Gabriel's office door—or what stood for a door, a wispy curtain of heavenly fabric. I chuckled bitterly. Gabriel was all about open-door policies. Unless you crossed him. Then it was more of a close-the-door-on-your-face policy.

"May I come in, Gabriel?" Without waiting for permission, I stepped inside his large office space. He was bent over some scrolls with a magnifying glass. If it weren't for his coloring, all snowy-white skin, hair and even clothes, I would've taken him for one of those old-school detectives of literary tradition.

His head snapped up, his pale blue eyes slightly out of focus and a rather surprised expression on his face.

"I didn't mean to interrupt, but I was wondering…. You look really busy, so I thought you may want me to grab you a mocha caramel latte from the coffee shop." *Nicely done.* Gabriel loved his fancy caffeine. The kind not available in the vending machines.

He blinked a few times as if stunned—truth be told, I'd never shown this kind of kindness toward him before—and licked his lips. "That would be very nice, Sky. Thank you." He thrust his hand into his pocket looking for money.

"No, my treat." I shook both my head and hand enthusiastically. "I've been nothing but a pain lately. It's only fair that I do something nice for you." *Okay. Don't go crazy or he'll be suspicious.*

Gabriel was shocked into silence and waved a thank-you and goodbye at me. That was all the permission I needed. I practically flew out the door and down the path to the community center. The building was one of my favorites because it was wholly constructed of heavenly glass, even the floors. No matter where you were in the building, it was as if you were floating in the clouds. It was the closest feeling I could licitly get to flying these days. The coffee shop was on the farthest corner of the building, but I had another stop first.

I dropped into one of the comfortable stools in the translator booths and didn't waste any time firing up the machine. It was a weird contraption that resembled a fax machine. You either inserted the paper with the text to be translated into a slot or sent the machine a message with it. I punched some numbers on my phone and waited for the telling pinging sound that the translator had received the message. It normally took only a few seconds for it to spit out a translation, and I was not disappointed. In less than a minute I had a fresh-out-of-the-oven translation of the cryptic note on Gabriel's desk.

I didn't want to delay, so I slid it into my pocket and rushed to the coffee shop to order the archangel's favorite drink. While I waited for the barista, I played with the piece of paper inside my pocket. I wasn't sure why, but I was convinced it had something to do with Caleb's situation. Gabriel only used Seraphic when he wanted to keep something secret and away from prying eyes and ears. I couldn't wait to read it.

Gabriel was overjoyed with the offer of the drink, if a little suspicious—he kept looking at me from the corner of his very blue eyes. He offered to pay for it one more time, but I turned him down. I owed him—or so I told him. He thanked me again and dismissed me from his office to go back to examining the scrolls. I strolled down to my desk, purposely making a big show of my lack of hurry so as not to alert Ms. Cranky-Pants. I shuffled through some of the piled documents on my desk, pretending to work, and when I was certain no one was looking, I inserted the translation into one of the files so I could read it without attracting anybody's attention.

Even though my brain was begging to read it fast, I took my time. I wanted to truly understand what it said, especially if it were about Caleb. For once, I didn't allow my lack of impulse control to rule over my common sense. The first couple lines had nothing interesting or telling, but then I saw Caleb's name written in the same paragraph as Samael's.

A cold shiver went through me. That couldn't be good. Samael was a dark angel whom many called "the blind one." Not because he couldn't see, but because he was virtually blind to anything decent and good. He had no conscience or qualms about doing the wrong thing; in fact, he thrived on evil.

Should Samael be inclined to take Caleb Pierce's life, the Department of Heavenly Collections would turn a blind eye. Due to an unavoidable glitch in the system, Mr. Pierce missed the date of his own death and is now a walking embarrassment for the department. I would be truly appreciative if both our departments would collaborate to bring this matter to a satisfying conclusion.

By the end of the note I shook uncontrollably. Only a thread of leftover sense—and my angel DNA—prevented me from flying to Gabriel's office and strangling him. How could an angel of good be so deceptively evil? How could he even consider such a move? Collaborating with the Other Side. Was the big boss aware it was happening? My best guess was no. I couldn't—wouldn't—believe the boss would ever be okay with such a thing. I had never liked the archangel very much, but I believed he would do the right thing always. That his angel heart would prevail in the end. Everything I had always believed had been destroyed. I was working for an evil angel.

When Gabriel left later that day, I was still sitting at my desk, absently shuffling papers. Cranky Amy left soon after, throwing curious glances at me. I wanted to scowl at her but had no energy left. Ironic that the hyperactive angel didn't have the energy to even stand up and walk home.

Tessa, another angel who worked in the maintenance department and often had to deal with my broken wings, came by my desk on her way out. "Are you feeling all right?" She seemed worried. Tessa was one of the very few angels who treated me with a modicum of respect. I think she felt sorry for me, always being mocked and ostracized. "You don't look well."

Angels didn't get sick much, other than a hangover

once in a while from too much ambrosia and, on the rare occasion, what went for a cold in Arcadia. I shook my head in denial. "I'm fine, Tessa. Thank you for the concern. Just tired." Which was a pretty outrageous statement considering we didn't get tired ever.

The tiny, big-bosomed angel clicked her tongue like an old woman and humored me. "Go home, young Sky. Get some rest." Then she left, throwing me a few more worried glances as she headed out.

I was spent, but not because of physical tiredness. My heart bled. All my convictions and values had been wiped out in a single move. The ones I thought I would trust to do the right thing weren't what they seemed. My whole world had collapsed. If I couldn't trust an archangel to do what was right, who could I trust? I suddenly longed for something I had never had: a friend, a sibling, a lover. Someone in whose arms I could hide and weep.

Sitting there wouldn't help me, or Caleb for that matter. He was in great danger. Samael was not someone to be trifled with; he was dangerous, cruel and ruthless. Caleb didn't die in that accident, so I was sure there would be another waiting for him down the road. Samael wouldn't rest until he saw his charge dead and his soul most likely harvested by the wrong side. I had to do something. But what exactly?

Eventually I dragged myself home, dropped on my sofa, and covered my eyes with my arm. *Think, angel. Think.* My brain was muddled with so many thoughts and revelations I couldn't think straight. If my brain was confused, my heart was pulling toward Earth and that hospital where Caleb was slowly healing from injuries that could've killed him. Injuries I now knew had not been accidental. No wonder he couldn't remember ever picking up his bike from the shop. He must've been placed on that bike by Samael right before crashing into a car. Caleb had been plucked from the streets of Boothbay Harbor like a pawn in a chess game and dropped in the middle of an ongoing accident.

I need to be with him. Now.

Uncaring of who might see me, I left my house and dropped off the Edge as soon as I reached it. I didn't care about my speed anymore. Let them catch me being reckless. Let them hand me to the big boss for disciplinary action. Urgency burned in my chest, a fear that if I didn't get there soon enough, it would be too late.

I may have broken the sound barrier on my way there. I set down with a great cloud of dust from the dirt in the back of the hospital, shook myself off, and ran inside. Caleb's bed was empty. I felt as if someone had taken a hard punch to my gut. *Oh God, no!*

"You're looking for the young man who had the motorcycle accident?" It was one of the ICU nurses. I nodded, incapable of talking. "He's been moved to the third floor. Room 108."

The poor nurse almost fell when I wrapped my arms around her in a big bear hug. "Thank you." I left her a little shell-shocked and ran up the stairs to the room where Caleb was alive and well. Tempted to just crash in, I thought better of it and knocked, rapping a happy rhythm on the painted wood.

Joan opened the door, and as soon as she saw it was me, she threw herself in my arms. "Sky, so happy you're here. They moved him out of the ICU yesterday. Where were you?" *Having my whole world crushed like a bug.* "He's been asking about you."

Is that a little tap dancing my heart's doing inside my chest?

She was still holding me when we entered the room. Caleb was half sitting on the bed, a few less tubes poking out of him than two nights before. "You're looking better," I said, aware of the silly smile stretching my lips and wrinkling the corners of my eyes. "You look alive."

Caleb laughed. I noticed he was clean-shaven, allowing for a better view of the big gash and scratches across his face. "Barely." He looked at his sister. "Get us some coffee, squirt."

"Just because you're sick does not make you the boss of me." The protest belied the grin on her face and the arms crossed over her chest. Caleb attempted batting his lashes and pouting comically. She cracked. "All right. I'll be back."

I was still standing by the edge of the bed, unable to take my eyes off Caleb. "I probably should let you rest...."

"No." The quickness of his reply startled me. The smile was gone from his lips, but his eyes were warm. "I'm so glad you came back."

Pitter-patter, pitter-patter went my heart. "Why wouldn't I?"

He motioned for me to sit on the edge of the bed, closer

to him, and I obeyed gladly.

"You've just met us. Why would you care?" *Because I'm in love with you, fool.* "We don't have any family left. I owe you big for being there for my sis." He lowered his voice. "And for me."

"She made me feel like I was part of the family, Caleb." The truth was often the easiest way to hide secrets. "I'm the one who's grateful. I don't have much of a family either."

"Thank you for taking care of her. It means a lot." He looked down at my hand resting close to his on the bed.

I gulped. Was I reading too much into his words? He was probably just grateful I hadn't left Joan alone. Still, it was heartwarming to hear him say it. "My pleasure, Caleb." I smiled and lowered my eyes.

Silence enveloped us, my fingers tantalizingly close to his, my eyes stubbornly glued to the bed.

"Joan really likes you. I'm a little jealous, in fact."

My head snapped up. What did he mean by that? To my great frustration, his eyes revealed nothing.

"Jealous of what?" I couldn't help myself. I had to ask.

"That she got to spend all that time with you while I was unconscious."

I tried to say something, anything, but my voice caught in my throat. I leaned over to kiss him. My eyes couldn't leave his. My brain was fighting my heart but losing. I needed to taste him again, make sure he was real. Make sure he was really there, flesh and bone, that I hadn't dreamed this whole thing.

My lips never made it to their target as Joan walked in,

juggling three cups of coffee. "Mercy. I leave for a second and you guys start making out?" Heat swept through my face and neck, and I dropped my eyes to the floor. "I'm kidding, Sky."

Caleb sought my hand with his. "You're cute when you blush," he said in a barely audible whisper. I stole a glance at him from the corner of my eye and smiled. The corner of his mouth was turned into a wicked little curl. "Joan has a gift to embarrass every guy who dares come close." His voice was audible again, and Joan turned to frown at him. "I think she's jealous that I seem to attract better-looking guys than she does."

Putting the coffee cups down abruptly, she grabbed an empty Styrofoam cup and threw it at him. Her aim was impeccable, hitting Caleb right between the eyes.

"Ouch. Is this how you treat your invalid brother?" His laughter was contagious. Before I realized, I was laughing along. Joan fought it, trying to look angry without much success.

Forgetting for a moment the fear from just an hour or so before, I allowed myself to be lulled by the warm feeling of belonging. Both brother and sister seemed to welcome me as an old friend, and I found that I loved it. We sat, talked, and joked around for a couple hours, sipping on the strong coffee Joan magically produced periodically. After a while, I noticed Caleb getting tired. His eyes were heavy with sleep and his voice became slightly slurred. I had seen it many times before. Dying wasn't that different from falling asleep, after all.

"Caleb needs to sleep for a while," I whispered to Joan as I coaxed her out the door, closing it behind us. "Let's go into the waiting room and let him be for a while."

She and I sat on the comfortable chairs in the waiting room, talking in whispers and getting to know each other better. She had a lot of questions about angels, and I wasn't sure whether to be amazed, scared, or plain amused that she truly believed in my angelic origins without question. I answered what I could and skirted around what I couldn't. Soon, her eyes began to close as well. I stood and helped her stretch on top of the couch, then covered her with the blanket we had dragged with us from Caleb's room and watched her for a few minutes while she drifted off to sleep. She was so tiny it was easy to think of her as a child, even though technically she was an adult. That Caleb felt he still needed to sacrifice his own life to take care of her was suddenly totally understandable to me. And also perfectly endearing.

Missing the sight of Caleb already, I left Joan to sleep and padded back to his room. The door was ajar and a little red alarm went off in my head. Cautiously I opened it and peeked inside. The dark silhouette of an angel was leaning over Caleb, doing something with his IV.

"Samael!" The yell came out unwarranted.

The fallen angel turned his perfect face to me, surprised at first, but then a malicious, dangerous smile stretched over his lips and worked its way to his black eyes. "Sky, I presume." His voice was melodious, strangely entrancing like the call of the sirens. "Came to save your charge? A little late, I'm afraid."

Terror filled my veins and without thinking, I ran toward the dark angel.

With a shimmer, he was gone before I reached him.

I stared at Caleb, not knowing what to do. Everything seemed to be okay. Quickly, I surveyed the tubes coming in and out from him, the IV, and the bag with the fluids Caleb needed to sustain his body. A reddish tint caught my eye. The liquid in the lower part of the IV tube had a different color from the one in the bag. It was very subtle; a human eye would probably miss it, but my celestial eyes could see it clearly.

Faster than I had ever moved, I pulled the needle from Caleb's arm just as the alarm on his heart monitor went off.

I'm too late!

***

A KISS

I'm not sure when I made the decision. Maybe it was the moment I saw life fleeing from Caleb's broken body. Maybe it was when I heard the agonizing scream that escaped Joan's throat when she walked in the room a few seconds later. Maybe I had already decided. Whatever it was, I was done. I wasn't going back to being Gabriel's lackey.

I held the elfin girl in my arms while she cried tears of unmeasurable pain. My eyes were dry. Inside there was anger, swelling like a malevolent balloon, filling me with its noxious fumes and making me gag. Angels weren't built to handle the ills of wrath. Within the room, behind closed doors, an army of doctors and nurses struggled to save Caleb's life. I hated myself for not knowing what kind of poison had been injected into his bloodstream, but one of the doctors had quickly identified it after I mentioned the reddish tint I noticed in the IV fluid. We were removed from the room and kept outside, closely watched by a ward nurse with sympathetic eyes.

Time seemed to have lost its contours. We were either waiting for hours or mere seconds—I couldn't tell the difference anymore. When a doctor finally emerged from Caleb's room, wiping his brow, I found I had lost my power of speech. That growing balloon had swelled inside of me until I was suffocating. Joan looked up from my shirt where she had buried her face. "How's…?" She couldn't finish the question.

The young doctor offered us a tired smile. "He's going to be okay." A great flood of emotion went through me and left me weak in the knees. Unable to control it, I dropped to the floor, bringing Joan with me. From the tightness of my chest, a wail of relief—or perhaps grief—rose and escaped.

It was Joan's turn to comfort me, her arms encircling my neck as she pulled me against her. "It's okay, Sky. He's going to be okay."

After allowing us a few moments of silence, the doctor spoke again. "We were able to stop the toxin in his bloodstream just in time. He won't suffer any side effects from it."

Tears burned my skin as they rolled down my cheeks and pooled around my mouth. I was relieved, happy, but also so very angry at myself. This was all happening because of what I had done. If I had let Caleb meet his maker when he was supposed to, he wouldn't be in danger now. He'd be in a good, happy place where he'd be cherished and rewarded for the way he led his life on Earth. Instead, he was being sought out by a cruel dark angel and in danger of being carried to rot in Hell.

Amid my grief, I almost missed it. "He's awake and asking for both of you."

Did he say "both of you"? Is Caleb really asking me to his side? I swallowed the tears, wiped my face with my sleeve, and got back on my feet. My legs still felt wobbly and I leaned all my weight on tiny Joan, who supported me like a champion.

Caleb was half sitting, propped up by a couple pillows. He was a little paler but didn't seem any worse than before the incident. His face opened up in a beautiful smile as soon as he set eyes on us. My legs were suddenly rejuvenated, as if those eyes had some kind of healing power. Good thing too, for Joan left me suddenly to run into the arms of her brother. I was tongue-tied. What was there to say to the guy you loved, who had just been poisoned by an evil angel? Not that he was aware of that, but still.

"It's been an interesting few days, hasn't it?" Caleb was actually chuckling as if he had been told a great joke rather than almost killed. Joan was gesturing me to come closer.

"I'll have a lot of great stories to tell my nieces and nephews when this one decides to give me some."

How can he be so cavalier about it? Or is he only being strong for Joan's sake?

The young woman was busy making sure her brother was comfortable, fluffing pillows and tucking in blankets. "For God's sake, sis," Caleb exclaimed, "will you stop fussing over me? I'm alive and have no intention of dying any time soon." I swallowed hard, still unable to say anything. "Be a sweetheart and get me some of that awesome coffee you can ferret out of this hospital, will you?"

I could see the hesitation in Joan's posture and stepped forward to volunteer to go in her place, but Caleb's warning glare stopped me in my tracks. He wanted her to go. "Please, sis." Joan shrugged in resignation and walked out, mumbling something under her breath.

As soon as she was out of the room, Caleb gestured for me to close the door and approach the bed. Curious and more than a little nervous, I did as requested. Much to my surprise, he held my hand and pulled me forward until I was sitting so close to him I could feel his body heat. My heart began the frantic drumming it always did when in close proximity to Caleb. I was still unable to speak.

"The doctors told me you were the one who sounded the alarm."

Hell, what do I say? "There was an evil angel over your bed?" Would he even believe me? Maybe before, when he still remembered me as an angel, but now?

He pulled me closer until I could feel the warmth of his

breath on my face. My own breathing accelerated as if I had run a marathon. My hand, still cocooned in his, was hot and tingly, and my gut—well, I wasn't even sure what my insides were doing. "Yes, it was me." I had finally found my voice, shaky and hoarse as it was.

Caleb's tantalizing lips curved in a smile. The handsome devil was enjoying my panic. His left hand gripped the front of my T-shirt and pulled me even closer. Our lips were mere nanometers apart, our breaths mingling in an intoxicating dance.

"Are you going to kiss me? Or do I have to get a doctor's note first?"

I lost it. My mouth came crushing down on his, hungrily tasting the lips I had been dreaming of for weeks now. He tasted like I remembered—ambrosia that went straight to my head. I felt drunk, my body quickly responding to the touch of his tongue inside my mouth, the suckling of my thirsty lips. His hand, flattened against my chest, burned my skin through the thin fabric of my shirt. I forgot where I was, who I was. The stars stopped shimmering and the world came to a halt. For a few seconds, all that existed was Caleb and me entangled in that kiss.

"Hell and tarnation!" Joan was quickly picking up some of my colorful angelic vernacular. "You're worse than teenagers in heat. You just came back from the dead, Caleb. Again! Can't you wait until you're on your feet?"

We disconnected and, dazed and flushed, stared at Joan who had entered the room unnoticed. She set the coffees on the tray at the bottom of the bed and placed her hands on her hips. "And you, Sky Heavensent, you should be ashamed of yourself. My brother needs his rest, not to be aroused to an inch of his life."

Heat once again covered me from head to toe. The little elf had a gift to make me blush. I stole a glance at my conspirator and was met with the most brilliant of smiles and a squeeze of the hand.

"Thank you," he mouthed as he caressed my hand with his thumb. I wasn't sure whether he was thanking me for saving his life again or for the epic kiss we had exchanged. Maybe both.

I smiled back, happiness replacing the mire of my previous anger. I had this sudden, ridiculous urge to run around like a crazed teenager, yelling, "OMG, he kissed me!" I licked my lips instead and was immediately rewarded, Caleb following the movement of my tongue and inhaling sharply. My smile widened to the point that I'm sure I looked like an idiot, but I couldn't help it. For the time being, I was filled with a new and exciting sense of hope.

Later, when it was time to go, I was torn. I knew I was no longer going to do Gabriel's bidding, but I was also smart enough to understand that as long as I was working at headquarters and the archangel was unaware of my dealings with Caleb—which may not have been the case anymore since Samael had recognized me—I was in the optimum position to get intel on what was going on. And hopefully stay one step ahead.

That knowledge didn't make my departure any easier though. I wanted to stay with Caleb and Joan, but I knew

I couldn't.

"I have to go. My boss doesn't take me being late lightly."
I threw a longing glance at Caleb, who smiled back at me.

"You're coming back, aren't you?" Joan seemed agitated
at the thought that I might not. "I like you, and you bring a
smile to my stupid brother's face."

Caleb's eyes wrinkled as he shook his head and frowned.

"I'll come back as soon as I can," I promised. "I've
grown to like you as well, squirt."

A smile stretched across her lips.

"Yeah, she does grow on you eventually—kind of like
mold." Caleb's remark was answered with a glare. He
laughed and turned his eyes to me. "Do come back. We have
some… unfinished business." He winked and my insides
melted.

I flew as slow as I could on my way back to Arcadia. The
sun was rising, its bright rays piercing through the clouds in
an awe-inspiring shower of light reflecting what I felt deep
inside. As an angel, I carried joy within me at all times, but
the sad side of my job had been creeping in and settling
sourly into my heart of late. Little tendrils of doubt and
sadness that had grown like ivy and encircled my soul to the
point of suffocation.

Deep in thought, I didn't notice the small group of angels
waiting for me at my door. They all carried the fiery swords
of the angelic police, and as soon as my eyes met their hard
and cold stares, I knew I was in big trouble.

PUNISHED

IMPRISONED

"I haven't done anything wrong." Technically that wasn't true. I had indeed broken one golden rule—or two—of my angelic duty. But speaking in terms of morality, I really hadn't done anything wrong. "Gabriel, you know that, as much as I'm clumsy and impulsive, I always do what's right. Isn't our seraphic duty to protect and love the humans in our charge?"

Gabriel wiped his face with a big hand and sighed deeply. He was annoyed. Seriously and dangerously annoyed. "Not if your duty is to harvest his soul." He paced on the other side of the rectangular table separating us. The angel cops had chained my wrists to the table, so my movement was limited. "You not only revealed yourself to and saved someone whose time on Earth was up, but then you proceeded to visit that same individual and are now standing between him and the forces of Heaven."

"Don't you mean *Hell*?" Beyond angry, I had lost my common sense. "You sent Samael to kill him. You're an angel. You're incapable of killing, of causing human suffering, so how can you justify such a cowardly and evil move?"

Gabriel leaned across the table. "I did not send a dark angel to kill anyone." He spoke through his clenched teeth, his normally even-colored face scarlet. "I don't know where you get your information, but I would never do something like that."

"Oh really? So who sent Samael to Caleb's hospital bed?" Spittle flew out of my mouth. "I was there, Gabriel. I saw him. I saw him injecting poison into Caleb's veins. I saw the note on your desk. I know it was you who commissioned him to kill the human."

Gabriel flinched at my last words. Was it possible he didn't know about it?

The archangel straightened up, pulled down on his shirt, and licked his lips. There was a momentary hesitation, as if he were trying to decide what would be the best thing to do, but before I knew it he had called two of the guards into the room. "Clip his wings and take him to isolation. No one—I repeat, no one—is to visit him, feed him, or talk to him other than me. Understood?"

Hyperventilating now that the words "clip his wings" had been uttered, I tried in vain to free myself from the chains holding me to that table. The guards came from behind me and coaxed my wings to retract and then—much to my horror—clamped them with a seraphic lock. The lock didn't cause any pain beyond being uncomfortable, but I was unable to unfurl and use my wings. Crushed, I was unchained from the table and dragged forcibly into the isolation chamber of Arcadia's police station.

Crime was virtually nonexistent, so the prison cells were mostly small rooms used to keep angels guilty of minor trespasses with barely any security at all. The isolation chamber was a different matter. It was reserved for those of us who had fallen and served as a kind of waiting room between Heaven and the other side. Wings were clipped to prevent the fallen angels from fleeing until such time as emissaries of darkness came to get them. It didn't happen often, and I had never expected it to happen to me.

The guards left me by myself in the small, all white room and locked the door behind them. I sat on the floor, leaning against the wall in disbelief. Was Gabriel really going to turn me into a dark angel because I did something good? Yes, I had broken a rule, but it wasn't the same as a mortal sin. I had done nothing evil, nothing that would warrant my change of status.

Tears burned behind my eyes, but I refused to free them. Gabriel wouldn't get the satisfaction of seeing me terrified out of my wits and heartbroken. I was never going to see Caleb again. Even worse, I would be doing the bidding of evil instead of good. For the first time in my very long life, I entertained thoughts of self-destruction, although I wasn't even sure if it were possible for an angel to commit suicide. Nothing scared me more than the idea of becoming a dark one.

Something startled me. A noise. A soft scratching sound at first, soon growing in crescendo to the point that I realized it was the screeching of a human being. A sound like that could mean only one thing—pain, and lots of it.

I jumped to my feet, my wings sore from the restrictive lock, and looked around me. I couldn't see much other than the bland walls of my prison staring back at me like bored ghosts. Another loud, heartrending screech filled the empty space and bounced off the walls. Where was it coming from?

As if from the edges of a dream, a figure appeared. No, two figures. One walking erect and with wings proudly unfurled behind him, the other slumped, nearly dragging across the floor. My heart stuttered like the faulty exhaust in a car.

"Caleb!" *It can't be. How could Caleb be in Arcadia? In this isolation booth? And why?*

The angel half dragging him approached, his step sure and almost cocky, and I saw his face. It was Samael. I swallowed hard and yelled his name. The dark angel locked eyes with me and smiled, a malevolent bloodcurdling stretch of the lips that reached his eyes as pure evil.

"If it's not the disobedient angel of death." His velvety voice scratched my ears as if wrapped in barbed wire. "I brought you some entertainment."

With a wide curve of his arm, Samael threw Caleb onto the floor in front of him where he lay still and crumpled like an old blanket. What had Samael done to him?

"Caleb! Are you all right?" My scream was met with no reaction, and my chest ached with the panic the silence caused.

The dark angel took a couple steps forward and kneeled

before Caleb. "Sweet human." He was cooing like a mother to an infant child. My stomach heaved. "Sweet little human. You must wake up. I have plans for you, and it's no fun when you're asleep."

I tried to move but found that my feet were glued to the floor, heavy as if attached to blocks of concrete. "What did you do to me?" I yelled at Samael, angry and frustrated.

"A simple paralyzing spell. It will wear off once I leave." There was no such thing as a paralyzing spell. Or was there? I didn't know anything anymore. Samael kicked Caleb gently at first, then harder when he didn't move. "Get the fuck up, human shit! I command you."

To my surprise and dismay, Caleb began moving and moaning. "Caleb, don't…." *Don't what? What could Caleb do against the evil angel?*

Samael waited for Caleb to get on his feet and then kicked him, his angelic boot rising up in the air and hitting him straight on the chin. Caleb's head was thrown backward as if he were a rag doll. I watched as blood flew out of his mouth and arched up in the air before plummeting to the immaculate white floor. Before Caleb could recover enough to fight back, Samael held his shoulders, forced Caleb to bend slightly forward, and then, raising his knee, savagely aimed it at my love's stomach. I heard the sickening sound of bone meeting flesh and watched helplessly as Caleb vomited blood.

"You're going to kill him." It sounded weak even to my ears, but I stood totally powerless to what was happening. I could only pray it would stop.

Samael cackled. "Not before I have some fun with this sweet piece of mortal meat. I wonder if he tastes good." The angel gripped Caleb by the throat and crushed his mouth to his. Caleb struggled against the forced embrace, and I whimpered in pain. When Samael finally released him, the angel's lips, drenched in blood, stretched in a sinister smile. "I see what attracts you to this human. He is fucking delicious."

"Leave him alone. Take me instead. Please." I was hysterical as I struggled against the invisible force holding me down.

Samael stepped closer, dragging the now unconscious body of my love behind him. "I will with one condition." His voice was a whisper and yet it pierced my ears like a scream.

"What? What do you want from me?" I was yelling and crying, my voice cracking in despair. "I'll do anything you want. Anything." I meant it.

The dark angel dropped Caleb and tilted my chin up with a bloody finger. "I get to turn you to the dark. You'll be my dark minion for the rest of your angelic life."

I dropped to my knees, sobs echoing in my chest. *No, not this. Anything but this.* But I knew I would do it. For Caleb. I allowed myself to drop even farther until my forehead hit the floor with a heavy thump.

I woke up drenched in tears and the smell of fear. Nothing had been real. It was only a nightmare. Aware that I should be relieved, anxiety grew within me instead. What if it were a prophetic dream? What if what I'd witnessed in my sleep were a reflection of the future?

I have to get out of here.

Time passes very slowly when you have no point of reference. The artificial light inside the blindingly white space didn't give any clues as to what time of day or night it was. My mind was full of bad things, things that could be happening to Caleb and his sister as I sat there, locked inside that room with my wings clipped. My wings ached under the pressure of the clamp, and my chest ached with each beat of my bleeding heart. I was lost.

When the telltale clank of the heavy door lock echoed through the small empty space, I flinched as if in pain. They were coming for me already. *Should I try to fight them? Is there even any sense in doing that? Where are you, God, when I need you the most?* I shuffled my feet and squeezed myself against the wall, hoping some magic door would open behind me and swallow me whole. Instead, I watched with surprise and some level of curiosity as Gabriel himself came through the open door, his finger in front of his lips, tiptoeing like a thief.

My lips opened in a question, but the archangel shushed me with his finger. Still scared, I stood up and waited for Gabriel to approach me. "Turn around quietly." His voice was a mere whisper but left no doubt he expected to be obeyed. I did as he told me, and I felt his cold hands on my back followed by an awesome sense of relief as my wings clamp came loose.

Gabriel released me. Why?

When I turned back around to face him, he gestured for

silence again. "Listen carefully, Sky." His voice was even quieter. "I did not request Samael, or anyone for that matter, to kill or hurt your human. In fact, until you mentioned it, I had no idea that had happened. All I did was erase his memory of you as per regulations. Something's wrong here." He sighed. "I'm freeing you. I gave orders for you to stay in isolation until further notice, so no one should notice your absence."

I blinked, not sure whether I was dreaming or this was actually happening. "But Gabriel, where am I supposed to go?"

Gabriel sighed. "Don't be an idiot, Sky." Well, this was no dream. Gabriel was back to being his usual asshole self. "Go to Earth. Hide. I'll contact you as soon as I can, and we'll talk. I fear there is something…." He looked for the right words. "Something very bad is happening here, and I need to find out what. You'll help me." It wasn't a request but an order. Though if it were true that he had nothing to do with this terrible mess, then I was very happy to help him find out who was behind it. "Will you do that for me?"

I nodded. "I will do that for Arcadia, for all of us angels of light." And for Caleb and Joan, but I didn't think he wanted to hear that.

"While on Earth, you must keep an eye on your human and protect him." Now there was something I could get fully behind. "You cannot allow him to be caught by the other side. He has a good soul. When he dies, he's expected on our side."

"I promise I will do my best."

"No! You have to do better than that. Your best is just not enough." *Man, he can be a real douche!* "For once, young Sky, you need to excel. Can you do that?"

With a nod I sealed our deal. Emerging from the isolation chamber, I realized it was the middle of the night. "How long have I been locked here?"

"Two days. Go to the Edge and fly as fast as you can." He threw me a glance and frowned. "On second thought, don't rush. Accidents happen when you rush. Just get down there safely and without being spotted. Understood?"

Gabriel didn't wait for my answer before he took off at great speed, flying over the building and into the skies beyond it. I stood alone for a few seconds, trying to process what had happened. Was it true? Gabriel wasn't the culprit behind Caleb's attempted murder. Did he really not know anything about it, or was this an elaborate ploy to get Caleb and me into even bigger trouble?

Whatever the answer, the one thing I was certain of was I was going to see my love again. I ran to the nearest side of the Edge and threw myself off it, gliding down rather than flying for fear the flapping of my wings would be detected.

Upon my arrival at the hospital, dawn had broken and small tendrils of sunlight shone down on the gray buildings. I found Joan in the waiting room, her ear glued to her phone and her hands punctuating whatever she was saying. Amused, I half hid around the corner and listened in.

"He is so cute." Boyfriend talk, apparently. "Curly, golden blond hair, freckles across his nose and cheeks, and the most gorgeous blue eyes you've ever seen." Was she speaking about me? "Cal melts every time he walks in the room. I think my brother is in love." *Aww.* My chest swelled with happiness. "I hope he's coming back. We haven't seen him in two days."

It wouldn't be right to intrude on her private conversation—a little belatedly—so took a different path to Caleb's room. Remembering what happened the last time I saw him, anxiety grew inside of me and I sped up my step. Caleb was fast asleep. The doctors had removed his head bandages, and a great big scar left from the surgery was visible on the right side of his forehead. The stitches were still there, making the wound look like the cartoonish mouth of a Halloween scarecrow. His forearms were wrapped in bandages where he had suffered a severe road rash, but he was beginning to look healthy again.

Quietly, I tiptoed into the room and pulled a chair closer to the bed so I could sit and watch him sleep. He looked so peaceful in his slumber that all the anxiety of the past couple days dissolve. Caleb was doing well, and I was by his side where hopefully he would allow me to stay for a while. All was well with the world and the heavens above.

***

GOING HOME

"You could just flap your wings and take us both home in

the blink of an eye." Joan was very stubborn, I was quickly finding out. Her brother was being discharged from the hospital, and she was stressing everybody out.

"I've already explained to you that I can't use my wings right now." It was at least the tenth time I'd said it. I lowered my voice and glanced around to make sure no one heard us. "It's dangerous."

It was easy to forget she was almost eighteen when she crossed her arms like a bratty child not getting her way. "We could be safe and sound at home already, and yet here we are still waiting for the fucking taxi."

"First, don't use that language. Your brother would kill you, and me, if he found out I didn't say anything." I liked it better when she used my old-fashioned, cleaner expletives. "Second, your brother still can't remember I'm an angel, and I really don't want him to freak out on me." I looked around one more time. "And third, can you please keep your voice down when you talk about my angelic gifts?"

With a pout and loud puffing, Joan turned around and started walking back inside. "You two deserve each other. Prude and impractical."

We had been waiting outside the hospital for the taxi to take us all home, but the cool breeze blowing from the ocean was becoming uncomfortable. I followed her in and placed myself behind the glass windows to keep an eye out. The doctors and nurses were doing their last round of checks and paperwork while we waited for our ride. It had been almost a week since Gabriel had freed me, and I was none the wiser about who or what was behind Caleb's near demise. Of course, I was so excited about getting to know Caleb better that I hadn't done much to find out what was going on. I planned to change that now that he was going home and I wasn't as worried about all the people coming and going.

"Why don't you want to tell Caleb your secret?" Joan was like a dog with a bone. "He'd believe you, you know."

As scared as I was that Caleb would think I was crazier than a loon under a full moon, that wasn't why I was resisting coming out to him. If he found out I was an angel, how would I explain to him why I was still around? And why I was in such big trouble? I couldn't bring myself to tell him the truth, that he was supposed to be dead.

"Joan, I'm not going to tell him any time soon. Drop it already. What's it to you, anyway?"

"It doesn't seem right that Caleb doesn't know who you really are." Well, that bothered me a little too. "You know he believes in angels, like me. You guys could be so good together."

I shook my head with a chuckle. "Will you let us make that decision ourselves?" I pointed at the taxi pulling in by the door. "The cab is here. Let's get your brother."

Caleb was ready, sitting in a wheelchair with a big smile on his face. "Ready to go back home," he said as we walked in. "Sick of this hospital room." Bubbles of happiness floated up my throat at the sight of his gorgeous eyes. Would I ever get tired of them? "Stop staring at me and wheel me out of this hellhole." Interesting choice of words, but I got the idea and did as I was told.

There was such chatter coming from Joan sitting up front that both Caleb and I were content just sitting quietly in the back seat of the cab. It had been a long while since I'd ridden in one of these human contraptions, and I couldn't help feeling like a fledgling on his first flight. I was used to speed, but flying was a smoother ride; this was a lot bumpier and rougher. The novelty made it thrilling in its own humble way. My lips stretched to the max as I stared out the window at the sights zooming by.

We had just crossed the small bridge into Wiscasset when Caleb's hand covered mine on the seat between us. Surprised but delighted, I glanced at it and then up at him. Ever since that kiss to end all kisses in the hospital room a week or so before, nothing had happened to make me think Caleb even remembered it, much less was willing to pursue it further. His fingers told me a different story. Warm and strangely familiar, he caressed my hand as his palm cocooned mine. That simple touch sent little electric shocks up my arm and directly into my heart—and other not-so-sentimental parts of me. A small fire began inside of me and quickly spread to every corner of my body. How very unangelic of me. I had the sudden urge to rip his clothes off and show him exactly how I felt for him right there on the stained seats of that cab.

Where is this coming from?

Thankfully the taxi stopped abruptly, and I had to let go of his hand to brace myself against the back of the driver seat.

Joan turned around to us with a big smile on her face.

"We're home."

With both his sister's and my help, Caleb limped—more like hopped—his way from the car into the house. Joan deposited him gently on the couch as I went back outside to pay for the taxi ride. The house still had that cozy appeal of the first day. It was weird how much at home I felt there, but so it was. Full, unapologetic comfort.

"Coffee, anyone?" At both our nods, Joan rushed to the kitchen to prepare the brew.

Awkwardness filled the room. Where a few moments before I had been ready to get very naked with Caleb, I was now inexplicably shy. Not sure how to proceed, I stared at the floor, desperately seeking something to latch on to. Nothing came to me.

"Come sit by me." Caleb's melodious voice soothed my nerves. My muscles relaxed just enough that I could finally look at him without blushing. I sat beside him on the couch and smiled. "You look a little nervous." That was the understatement of the century. I didn't know what to say. "Thank you for being here."

In spite of my earlier resolve, heat climbed from my neck to my cheeks. Hell and tarnation, what was it about the man that made me so flustered? "I like being here." *Really? Of everything you could've said, you pick that? I might as well be Baby from* Dirty Dancing *with her watermelon comment.*

Caleb's laugh filled my ears like a song. "Good, because I like having you here."

Joan came back carrying a tray with cups and a carafe, her joy in having her brother back splashed across her pretty, young face. "So excited to have my two boys here with me."

"Since when did Sky become one of your boys?" Caleb pretended to be annoyed. "I thought I was your only one."

Joan stuck her middle finger up at him and poured him a cup of coffee. "You used to be, but now I have my angel as well."

My heart fell at my feet. What was she doing, telling him about me? I stared at her with what I hoped was a pointed look.

She didn't notice. "My sweet Sky." She left her coffee accessories behind and threw herself in my arms. "I can't thank you enough. You've been an angel." The little devil winked at me. She was having fun rattling me. I squeezed a little harder than necessary and she laughed. "Let me get you a cup of my heavenly brew."

I'm going to kill her.

Twilight immersed everything in a quiet, cozy glimmer of sorts. Caleb insisted on ordering Chinese, and we munched on crunchy noodles and dumplings in pleasant companionship. I found that talking to these two was as easy as if I had known them my whole life, and I didn't want to give it up. Ever.

"Where are you staying, Sky? You've never told me where you live." Caleb had dropped a bomb. I had never even considered that. Since angels didn't need much rest, I had been catching up on sleep curled up in the hospital waiting rooms, never once considering that I didn't have a place to stay anymore. The hospital had been my home for the past week.

The elfin girl saved me. "He's currently looking for a place. Sky moved here recently and was staying at a hotel until your accident." *Okay, I forgive you for the earlier tormenting.* "I thought he could stay here until he finds a place."

My head snapped up in surprise. "No, I wouldn't think of imposing on you guys like that. Especially with Caleb still recovering."

Caleb waved his hand. "Don't be silly. You're very welcome to stay with us for as long as you need." His lavender-green eyes pierced mine with their intensity. "It'll be wonderful having you here. Little Miss Muffet here needs to go back to school, and I'll be very lonely."

Was he flirting? It had been a very long time since I had done anything like that, and never with a human. My core contracted in excitement or fear. Maybe both.

"Are you sure? I really don't want to put you guys out." Except now I really wanted to stay. The smoky glance Caleb was throwing my way was all the incentive I needed.

Joan giggled, her laughter rising into the air and cascading all around us like little crystal bubbles. "Can't you see my not-so-subtle brother wants you around? Just say yes already and stop playing coy."

I must've blushed again because the room became very hot all of a sudden. "Yes, I will be very happy to stay. I have nowhere else to go. Thank you." That earned me another neck-breaking hug from Caleb's sister.

The house was small and they had no extra rooms, so

Joan set me up on the couch we had been sitting on. I didn't need much, but she insisted on providing me with blankets, pillows, and a change of clothes. "You won't sleep in your day clothes while you're my guest." She also magicked a new toothbrush. She was so excited I didn't want to tell her that I didn't need it since angels were gifted with permanently clean teeth. However, even angels couldn't go forever without a good shower, so when she offered me a towel and a bar of soap, I almost kissed her.

By the time I left the shower, Caleb had retired to his room and Joan was waiting for me in yoga pants and a T-shirt. "You look good," she said appreciatively. "And smell good too. No wonder Caleb can't take his eyes off you." Her pretty face, so different from her brother's, opened up in a generous smile. "So glad you're here, Sky. Good night."

I was alone in the living room, lit only by the small lamp on the end table. Unhurriedly, I looked around me. The old, mismatched furniture was as welcoming as an old friend. I entertained the idea of sneaking into Caleb's room and following through with my earlier fantasy, but the man I was in love with was recovering from a life-threatening injury and needed to heal.

I sighed and stretched my long body on the short sofa, neglecting to cover myself, and much to my surprise began to drift away to sleep.

FALLING AGAIN
WANTING

To my dismay, I found out that I was no Sherlock Holmes. I had been investigating the strange case of the dark angel for almost two weeks, and so far I was coming up empty— although I did have a great title for a mystery if I ever decided to become an author. On one hand, the fact that Samael or any of his cronies hadn't shown up to wreak havoc in Caleb's life was a relief. On the other, it also made me very nervous as to what they may be plotting.

Caleb was getting stronger every day, in spite of Joan's assumption to the contrary. He was able to walk around without much help and didn't require as many hours of sleep as before. The scar on his forehead was healing nicely, and the road burns on his face were faded. His arm, on the other hand, was still bandaged; the burns there had gone much deeper and were taking longer to heal. I watched him with fascination as he wobbled around the house, seemingly aimless but with purpose nevertheless. His hair had been shaved for the surgery and had grown back just enough to cover his scalp with a very dark, fuzzy layer. Sheltered beneath equally dark lashes, his unusual eyes glittered and shone like beams of light that filled me with longing.

Angels dated. Some, like my parents, mated for life and lived lives not unlike those of human couples. I'd had my romantic liaisons—far and between, it was true, but there nevertheless. Being the clumsy one, the "liability," didn't make me very attractive to other angels though. Angelic creatures treasured perfection, order, control. I was the perfect picture of everything flawed, chaotic, and out of control. Most of my dates had been angels going through a rebellious stage who thought they would enjoy a relationship with a wild one. They didn't.

In the relative solitude of my life, I had never felt anything like the longing I did every time I looked at Caleb. It scared me a little.

With Joan back in school, it was oddly quiet. Her incessant chatter filled the house with bubbling life, and I missed it. The silence provided an opportunity for my hyperactive brain to fill me with dread that this—whatever this thing with Caleb and Joan was—would be over too soon, that Samael would take Caleb. Fear that Caleb didn't and would never love me back.

"You have that look." Caleb's voice snapped me out of my reverie.

"What look?"

"The one that tells me you're a million miles away." He was leaning against the door frame, the corded muscles across his chest bulging slightly under the blue T-shirt. My breath quickened.

"I was thinking it's too quiet here without the elf around." With my heart playing a crazed drum solo, I tried to smile but probably frowned instead. I was so over my head.

Caleb took a few steps forward until he was standing right beside me, and I stumbled backward slightly as my legs turned to Jell-O. My famous angelic awkwardness came flooding back to me with a vengeance. Uncertain of where to put my hands or rest my eyes, I fumbled and almost tripped over a decorative basket behind me. Caleb reached out to brace me against a fall, and I found myself suddenly wrapped in his arms. The room became very hot, my throat desert dry.

"Do I make you nervous?" The question was a bit surprising considering our bodies were now so close I could feel the rhythm of his breathing. I blinked rapidly, a fluttering of tiny wings in my belly. Caleb chuckled softly. "There! You lost your voice. Why are you ill at ease around me?"

I wanted to reply, I really did, but my dry mouth wouldn't let me, and my thoughts had gone as fuzzy as the morning mist over the harbor. I may have stuttered something, but I couldn't be sure. Caleb looked at me amused, his hand still loosely wrapped around my waist. Then he did *that* thing, the one where he licked his luscious lips and upturned the corner of his mouth in a half smile. A shiver shook me from my toes to the top of my head. My hidden wings quivered in anticipation and I forgot all my earlier anxieties. I stepped forward until my body was flush with his, every hard ridge that was Caleb touching my hypersensitive body. I heard a soft moan and realized it was me. His bandaged arm followed the other one around me and pulled me closer, so close there was no way of hiding my reaction to his touch.

For someone who claimed not dating often, Caleb seemed a virtuoso of the art of seduction. His eyes trained on my mouth, begging me to kiss him, as he slid a hand down to press my lower body against his.

"What are you doing to me?"

Did I say that out loud?

Caleb laughed, a soft rolling sound deep in his throat. Our lips connected with a hunger that both pleased and shocked me. I wanted this man like I had never wanted anyone or anything in my life.

His tongue playing havoc with my senses, Caleb pulled me even closer and I decided at that moment that our clothes were in the way. I fumbled with the button on his jeans, never once allowing my lips to part from his. After a few seconds, I gave up on the pants and turned my attention to his T-shirt, holding on to the lower edges and pulling it over his head, throwing it across the room. Caleb pressed his lips to the crook of my neck and ignited a wildfire.

The angel in me had gone into hiding somewhere in the depths of my being, so it must have been the human part of me who noticed the scars and scratches across his chest and arms, the telltale signs that he was still recovering from a life-threatening accident.

What am I doing? Am I really considering having sex with a convalescent human? Where has my angelic sense gone?

Probably to the same place Caleb's shirt did.

"I'm sorry, Caleb. I wasn't thinking." I pushed myself away from him, my whole being protesting the separation. "You just had surgery and here I am…. Sorry."

Caleb looked a little dazed, as if waking up from a deep sleep and not being sure of what he was witnessing. "Are you really sorry?" His bare chest was making my decision to be sensible very difficult. He stepped closer again. I stepped back. "Come on, Sky. I'm fine. Healed almost completely." He pointed at his still very purple head scar. "I can handle it."

I moved backward a couple extra steps and twisted my hands in semi-agony. "No, it's not right. The doctors said complete rest for at least six weeks. It's been less than four weeks. Too soon."

Caleb wiped his face with a hand and sighed deeply. "Do you really not want to do this?"

My breath was still coming out in little spurts, my heart a stampede. "Yes. I mean no. I mean—hell!" I looked at him, all muscle and length, and my gut clenched in yearning. My voice went quieter. "I want you. Badly. But I also care too much about you and Joan and realize that giving in to my wanting right now could hurt you."

"And you don't want to hurt me." He was smiling that devilish smile of his.

I smiled too. "No, I don't care about that. What I don't want is to face Joan's wrath if you do get hurt." He burst out laughing and I followed suit. I loved it when his eyes crinkled at the corners. Before I could stop myself, I lifted my hand to his face. "Soon, I hope—"

The click of the door unlocking interrupted the moment. We both turned our heads to watch Joan come in with her backpack draped over one shoulder, keys in her hand, and an expression that betrayed mischief. Belatedly, I realized I still had my hand on Caleb's face and was immediately consumed by a rush of blood to mine.

Joan lifted an eyebrow. "Did I interrupt anything interesting?" With a long inquiring stare, she scanned us from head to toe. "Who am I kidding? The two of you must be the most boring of all young people. You're an embarrassment to the age group, really. While I'm in school, couldn't you at least have wild monkey sex in the living room?"

Caleb's earlier smile turned into a frown. "Watch it, girl! I may be young but I'm still your older brother."

The elfin girl huffed a little, threw her backpack into a corner, and passed us on the way to her room. "You mean geriatric brother, right?" She never stopped to see her brother's reaction to her words.

I looked at Caleb and he looked at me. As if by mutual agreement, we both tried to repress the laughter bubbling up our throats, but we couldn't. Joan was a pistol of a girl, and I had come to adore her. She might as well be my little sister.

I hope they never regret knowing me.

✳ ✳ ✳

ESCAPE

The bathroom was too small for my wings, but it was the only place in the house where I could freely stretch them out. Keeping them forever furled became very uncomfortable after a while, like wearing a pair of very tight shoes. Eventually you need to give your toes a little space. As I turned around, my right wing hit the shelf on the wall and a myriad of cosmetic containers fell to the floor, causing a racket. As I bent down to pick them up, my other wing whacked the blow-dryer off the counter. *Just don't move!* I followed my own advice and stopped for a moment, enjoying the sensation of my totally opened wings.

As I stood in the middle of the tiny bathroom in silence, I thought I heard the muffled sounds of crying. Both Joan and Caleb were home. I had left them on the couch arguing about what show to watch on TV. We had gone out for dinner at Caleb's favorite fast food place and now, stuffed with fries and burger meat, had decided on a laid-back night of TV binging.

I heard the sound again. I perked up my ears and was surprised to hear nothing. Caleb and Joan were anything but quiet when they bickered; the silence was deafening.

In a swift move, I furled up my white wings and opened the door. Suddenly my chest began hurting with a strange urgency, a premonition of sorts. My weak angel superpowers hadn't deceived me—as soon as I crossed the doorway, I saw Joan lying on the carpet, unmoving. Caleb was nowhere to be found, and the front door was wide open.

I knelt by Joan's still body, my heart beating a hundred

miles an hour, and cradled her in my arms. "Joan, honey. Wake up." As I tried to coax her out of whatever was ailing her, my gaze traveled to the door, pain crushing my chest. Where did Caleb go? Was he taken?

The elfin girl began moving in my arms and her eyes fluttered open. "Where's Caleb?" Her voice was hoarse and panicky. "They took him, Sky."

I brushed my hand over her hair, trying to calm her down. "Who took him?" The panic in my heart was rising and swelling like bread dough left in a warm room for too long. Somehow I knew the answer.

"An angel… but not like you." She sobbed into my arm. "He had black wings and evil eyes."

Not a surprise, but a shock nevertheless. "Samael," I whispered, anger and fear forming a knot in my throat.

"Where is he taking Cal?"

Joan's shaky voice made me swallow my fear. They needed me. It wasn't the time to panic and lose it.

"I have to go after him," I said, anxious to find Caleb but reluctant to leave her alone. She sat up and looked at me with a question in her swollen eyes. I sighed. "Before Samael takes him somewhere no one wants to go."

"What do you mean?" Joan seemed wide awake now. It didn't look like Samael or his lackeys had hurt her. He must have used a sleep hex on her, temporary slumber-on-demand, a common angelic trick.

"I've been trying to figure that out since his accident." Why lie? It wasn't as if Joan didn't know the truth about my kind.

"Are you telling me it was no accident?"

I nodded and helped her up from the floor. "Joan, I need to go before it's too late. Promise me you'll be okay, and keep that door locked while I'm gone." Not that it would keep her safe, not from the likes of Samael and his minions, but there wasn't much else I could do at the time. She nodded enthusiastically. I knew she would do anything to save her brother. "I don't know how long it'll take, but I'll do everything I can to bring him back safe and sound."

Rising on her tiptoes, my adopted sister kissed my chin. "I believe you. You'll bring him back, I know it."

I gave her a small smile, hoping her faith wasn't misplaced, and rushed to the door. Not daring to look back at her distraught face, I ran into the night, my wings fully unfolded and my toes already floating above the ground. For a fraction of a second, I wondered whether anyone would notice the shimmering of my presence. Pushing that fear into the back of my mind, I flew at full speed after the one I loved.

I couldn't be one hundred percent certain of where Samael was taking Caleb, but I was willing to bet it was to Hades, where the souls of the departed waited for transfer to the hellish realm of the dark angels. I headed there with a heavy heart. *Please, don't let him be dead.*

My love for speed was finally being put to some good use. Possibly the only thing I excelled at—being faster than any other angel, dark or light.

Hades wasn't far in angelic terms. Kind of like Neverland: second star to the right, and straight on till morning. The trick was to find the portal. For reasons that no one in Arcadia really understood, the location of the portal often changed. It was as if the dark angels wanted to prevent everyone from coming in uninvited, but then, who would ever want to go to Hades voluntarily?

My status as the outcast was an asset for once. No one paid attention to me, and my presence was often overlooked during personal and largely secretive conversations, so I had once overheard a conversation between Gabriel and Michael about how to find the portal without spending the rest of your long seraphic life looking for it. I searched for the telling disturbance of light, like the edges of an ocular migraine: a shimmering rainbow, faded but definitely visible to those paying attention.

With my wings flapping and my eyes performing a crazed scanning of the sky, I hadn't had much time to wonder whether Samael had simply taken Caleb or if he had—no, I couldn't think of that. He was alive. I could feel it in my bones.

From the corner of my eye I saw it, the wavering of light with a hue of pink and red. The portal, finally. Not giving my brain the chance to question it, I propelled myself as fast as my wings could carry me through the invisible gate to Hades.

I felt it before I could see it: the extreme heat, uncomfortable and sticky like a summer day in the tropics. The blue sky had vanished and what went for it in this place was reddish, spotted with threatening clouds heavy with lightning and rain. I wiped my brow, already covered in sweat, and looked around me. No one was in sight. At a distance, I could discern a structure of some kind, maybe a building. There was a pull inside my head as if Caleb was somehow telepathically communicating with me. Not for the first time, I wondered whether maybe a new bond had been created between us the moment I saved him from his death. Whatever it was, I followed my instincts and flew toward the building with renewed hope.

The closer I came, the greater the fear in my heart. The building—if it could even be called that—was huge, stretching as far as the eye could see. The top was hidden by the ominously thick clouds, and there were no windows anywhere. The surface of the structure seemed to be moving as if covered in millions of slimy, black slugs.

Before I got close enough to be seen, I stopped and studied the place. The moving surface was in fact some kind of viscous black and reddish material that oozed from the top to the bottom in big, slow globs. I searched for a door but couldn't find any. *There must be a way in.*

While I half crouched behind a dead bush, a couple of angels alighted close by. I watched in morbid fascination as they carried a screaming soul between them, none too gently. The black wings of the angels flapped around them, evil-looking but magnificent, as they dragged the terrified soul toward the side of the structure. Baffled as to where they were going considering I couldn't see an entry of any kind, I kept my eyes on the trio. They approached the oozing wall and walked straight through it as if it weren't there.

Immaterial walls, like the ones in Gabriel's office but opaque. On one hand, I was happy to have figured out a way in, but my stomach revolted against the very idea of walking through that wicked slime.

Bracing myself, I took a deep breath and rushed to and through the moving wall into—well, not exactly what I was expecting. Thankfully I had picked a good spot to enter the structure, for it took me to a small space half-hidden from the rest by a wall. The black goo I had passed through stuck to my feathers in spots, giving them the appearance of a snowy owl's wings.

The inside of the building wasn't very different from headquarters, but darker. Much darker. And not because there were dark angels and wicked souls crawling all over it. The artificial light bounced off black walls and furnishings, giving the whole space a sickly aura. There were angels everywhere, talking to each other, escorting—more like lugging—souls to what I guessed were holding cells of some kind. Where the Arcadia headquarters had open spaces with no barriers or walls, this place was a maze of narrow corridors with lots and lots of walls. An open area seemed to be the hub of the whole building while around its edges, corridors and doors took the dark angels and their charges to other, more hidden parts.

That's where I'll find Caleb.

Stealthily, I followed the angels carrying their charges in hopes they would lead me to the holding cells. After a few close calls, I managed to arrive at my destination undetected. The shock at what I was witnessing almost threw me to the floor. The room was narrow, but it stretched to impossible heights with walls lined with what looked like human-size glass capsules. The angels were placing the ghostly glowing souls into those capsules and locking them within. From where I was hiding, I could see the looks of agony on the faces of the unfortunate souls locked inside. They were like glass tombs, no room to move. According to what I'd learned in Angel Academy as a fledgling, they were made to stand for as long as it took for them to be released into the hands of the evil minions of the Dark One, the big boss of the dark side.

Every muscle in my body cramped at the thought that Caleb may be one of them. *No, he's alive. I can feel him tugging at my heart.* I scanned the room, trying to stay calm in spite of my accelerating heartbeat. The whole room was lined with the horrible capsules and seemed to pulsate with fear and pain.

It took me a while, but my eyes finally homed in on a small door, easily missed amongst all the rest. There was a weird-looking lock on the outside, like an air lock on a submarine door. My breath caught in my throat. That was it, I was sure. The only place where they could keep a live human being. I had heard rumors in the past of dark angels such as Samael or Lahash taking still-living humans to torture for sport. At the time those stories had been frightening, but now they froze me with horror. *What if Samael's torturing Caleb?*

I waited for what seemed like an eternity, crouched along the wall, scared that the angels lingering around would hear my galloping heart. The moment finally came when the creepy, giant room became empty and quiet, save the muted sounds of moaning coming from the soul capsules. Quickly, I made my way to the door and, grabbing hold of the wheel-like lock, braced my muscles to pry it open. The lock turned easily, and a whooshing sound of trapped air being released echoed through the large space. I cringed, but it wasn't the time to be afraid. I had to move quickly if I was ever going to rescue Caleb. The door swung open and I peeked inside, afraid of what I may see.

Caleb was curled up in a corner of the black room, and at the surge of light coming through the open door, he looked up with blind eyes. "Who's there?" What had they done to him? With relief I realized his eyes, immersed in total darkness for a while, were simply adjusting to the light. He blinked a few times as I approached quietly, afraid to make any sound. "Sky? Is that you?"

Forgetting he couldn't see very well, I placed a finger in front of my lips. "Shh. Don't say anything. They'll hear us." Caleb tilted his head like a bird. "The angels outside. We have to move fast. Can you walk?"

Caleb stood up, supported by the wall behind him. "Yes. My legs are a bit wobbly, but I can move."

We were about the same height, his six-odd feet matching mine, but he seemed shorter right then. I realized he was slightly bent at the waist as if something were bothering him. "What's wrong? Did they hurt you?"

Caleb shook his head. "No, I'm fine. Just cramping from sitting too long." I didn't believe him for a minute. I was very familiar with the body language of pain, and he was indeed in some kind of discomfort. There was no time to hesitate though, so I wrapped an arm around his waist and another behind his knees, preparing to carry him out. "Wait, wait," he exclaimed suddenly. "What are you? Am I a damsel in distress? And if so, where's your shining armor?"

I was in no mood to laugh, even if he seemed inclined to make light of the situation. "I don't have armor. But I do have wings." With those words, I unfurled them to their full extent and watched him briefly as his jaw dropped, his eyes rounding like an anime character's. Angels are strong, and I was no exception. My body may be slim, but my muscles were well-developed and capable of carrying extremely heavy weights. With a swooping motion, I picked him up in my arms and carried him out of the room. A quick survey of the capsule room told me no one was around, and after shutting the door behind me, I raced into the more sheltered space of the mazelike hallways. There I moved even faster, half crouched—as much as I could be with Caleb in my arms—all my senses trained on my surroundings, alert to any noise, any movement. The screwup in me wouldn't be allowed to mess it up this time.

Caleb tried to talk once, but I shushed him by placing my lips on his and literally speaking into his mouth. It was imperative he made no sound. He understood and remained as quiet as he could from then on.

Negotiating the twists and turns of the hallway leading to the main room wasn't easy. Every turn looked the same and many ended—as in a real maze—in dead ends. It took a lot longer than I had hoped, but eventually we arrived at the end of the maze. It was the hardest—and most dangerous—part of this rescue; to leave the slimy, dark structure, we had to come out of hiding for a few seconds and throw ourselves through a very visible wall. With my complexion and white wings, I stood out like a sore thumb. I looked around for inspiration and my eyes locked on the slimy material that oozed from the walls.

Gently, I set Caleb down. "Help me cover my wings and hair in this mess." I was already scooping handfuls and rubbing it all over my blond hair. "I can't reach the wings. You have to do it." For a fleeting second I cringed at the thought of the goop covering my pristine and glorious wings—my only pride and joy.

We finished our camouflage mission within a minute or so as Caleb needed no disguise, his black hair and dark clothes blending well with the rest of the building. "I'm going to pretend to be dragging you." I placed my hand under his arm with a viselike grasp and, gingerly at first, stepped into the main room, dragging him behind me. I kept my eyes—too blue not to be noticed—on the floor and walked faster toward the closest wall where I surrendered my hold on him.

"Follow me no matter what." I wasn't sure he heard my hushed voice, but when I determinedly walked through the oozing surface, he followed me without hesitation. As soon as we were outside in the overwhelming heat, I scooped him back into my arms and flew without as much as a look behind me. Space, and lots of it, was what we needed between us and that place.

The goop dripping from every inch of my wings weighed me down slightly, but we reached the portal in no time. On the other side, the air was lighter and more breathable, making my flight easier.

"You're an angel too?" It was the first time I'd heard his voice since rescuing him from the horrible sensory deprivation chamber, and it startled me. "Like the guys who took me?"

I found my voice, even if I was avoiding his eyes. "Not like them. They're dark angels. I'm an angel of light." Flying through the clouds made me shiver a little, the moisture in them sticking to my skin like spiderwebs.

"Why didn't you tell me?"

"Would you have believed me if I did?" *Besides, you already knew, fool.*

For a while, the only sound I could hear was the subtle flapping of my wings and not-so-subtle beating of my heart. Caleb was thinking. "Probably not. But then again, I have seen one of you before…."

"I know. Joan—"

His body tensed against my chest. "Joan! Is she okay? They did something to her."

"She's fine. They put her to sleep, that's all." Well, it was a little more complicated than that, but why explain? She was indeed in good health and that was all that mattered. I took a look behind me to make sure we weren't being followed. We weren't. I breathed a little easier. "Are you freaked out? About me being an angel?" *Please, don't be.*

His lips pressed against the bottom of my neck, and the

overwhelming heat returned in full force. "You have always been an angel to me and my sister." His warm tongue flickered across my skin, sending millions of tiny electric shocks through me. "The wings are new, but man, are they sexy."

I almost dropped him.

TOGETHER
Making Love

"Watch it, girl. You're going to pluck me like a chicken." Joan was busy cleaning my wings. Neither of us knew exactly what to use to remove that awful gunk from my feathers, but we figured what worked for the fuel-covered ocean animals should work for me as well. Once in a while she became a bit too enthusiastic and I would lose a feather or two. We were like the lizards of the heavenly world; we could grow back our wings almost overnight. Repairing them was more complicated.

"Stop fidgeting. This isn't easy, you know." To give her due credit, she was right. Joan was doing a great job and showing a facet of her personality I didn't know existed—her patient side. She cleaned each individual feather with the patience of a saint—which was largely overrated, by the way—and never once complained about how long it was taking.

Caleb, who had been napping in the living room, stared at us with a frown. We were in the kitchen, Joan standing by me while I sat on a barstool. We must have looked almost comical, me with half-white, half-black wings—and let's not even mention my poor hair—and she with a dripping sponge in one hand and a blow-dryer in the other. Norman Rockwell would've had a field day with us. I noticed Caleb was still slightly bent at the waist but chose not to say anything so as not to worry his sister.

"So, let me get this straight. Joan knew you were an angel all along?" He sat down on the next barstool, grabbing another sponge and joining his sister in cleaning my wings. The mere idea of his fingers touching my feathers made me shiver in pleasure.

"I'm not as thick as you." Joan never wasted an opportunity to ruffle her sibling's metaphorical feathers.

Caleb threw the wet sponge at her and an all-out sponge war began. By the time it was over, we were all soaking wet, as were the floor and every wall around us. My wings were whiter though.

While they were finishing the cleanup, I grabbed the bottle of Dawn and marched to the bathroom. "I'm going to take an old-fashioned shower and see if I can get rid of this gunk once and for all." No one protested.

There were still some blackish spots here and there, but after the hot shower I was fresh and cleaned of the evil goo. I had been careful to wash it all down the drain and then pour the bleach I found under the sink after it—there was no telling what that stuff could do. I dried myself with a large fluffy towel, put a pair of clean joggers on, and left the bathroom within a cloud of vapor mist.

Caleb was watching me from the end of the short corridor, his eyes devouring every inch of my body. My stomach clenched, as did my more intimate parts. I gulped, the first stirrings of desire taking a firm hold of me.

"Where's Joan?" My voice broke and stuck in my throat. If his eyes could do that to me, I trembled at the thought of what his hands could do.

"Study group for the next couple hours." Caleb uttered the words with a half smile. "And if I know her, ice cream afterward. We have the house to ourselves." Like a caress, his velvety voice brought a shimmer of heat to my skin.

"What do you propose we do, then? I was looking forward to a quiet movie afternoon." I'm not sure where I found the strength to make a joke. My whole body shook in anticipation of what his eyes were promising.

Caleb treaded forward, his eyes never leaving mine until he stood in front of me. "I can think of a thing or two we could do." He lifted his hand and swiped it slowly from the bottom of my neck all the way down my bare chest. I swallowed a moan and swelled at his touch. Lavender and green followed his hand down until his fingers dangled from the low waist of my pants, hooking into the drawstrings. A devilish smile stretched across his lips and crinkled the corners of his eyes. I loved that smile.

"Hell, Caleb. You're driving me crazy." I covered his hand with mine and brought it to my lips. "Are you sure you're okay for this?"

Fanning his fingers across my mouth, Caleb caressed my face, neck, shoulder, and down my arm. I felt as if I were glowing like a star. Incapable of standing still any longer, I slid my hand under his T-shirt, then across his sides and along his ribcage. To feel him shiver at my touch was as exhilarating as the fluttering of his fingers around the waist of my joggers.

With a groan, Caleb, hand flattened on my chest, pushed me backward until my back was against a wall. His lower body, crushed against mine, left no doubt as to how much he wanted me. There was no hiding my desire either as our bodies rubbed and tugged against each other. I pulled on his shirt and he raised his hands high above his head, inviting me to undress him. As I stripped him of the T-shirt—slowly, enjoying every inch of naked skin I revealed—my whole being vibrated as if a current of electricity raced through me. I hadn't felt so alive in a very long time, and I realized I missed it.

Our lips connected again in a hungry kiss. I couldn't get enough of his flavor, his heat. Our tongues entangled in a delicious, exciting dance. My muscles clenched and released to the rhythm of my heart beating at the speed of light.

Without realizing it, my feet floated above the ground, my white wings flapping gently as I gripped Caleb's waist, supporting him. He chuckled against my lips. "You've swept me off my feet. Literally."

I gently brought us down and pushed Caleb away from me just enough to look at his magnificent body. "I may be the angel, but you have a body that would put any angelic creature to shame." My fingers sought the button on his jeans and struggled with it. "I'm really bad with buttons." I laughed softly and almost cried out in relief when it finally came undone.

My hands were shaking as I began pulling his jeans down. Caleb stopped me, his hand covering mine and his eyes burning. "Let me." In a few seconds he was naked, and I was hyperventilating. *Get it together, angel. You've seen more than your share of naked people.* Which was true, of course. But they were mostly dead. Caleb was very much alive.

"May I?" So intent on soaking in the artwork that was Caleb, I almost missed his request. He had hooked his fingers in the drawstring of my joggers and was gently pulling the knot apart. Having lost my power of speech, I nodded, half-dazed.

Caleb followed my pants down, and I thought I would die of pleasure when he wrapped his lips around my arousal. I threw my head back and arched against his mouth in pure ecstasy.

"Holy shit, Caleb. I may explode." His hands were on my backside, caressing, bringing me closer. Afraid I couldn't handle it anymore, I pulled away. I needed to be even closer to him.

Shivering, I kissed him again, hard and long. Caleb whimpered against my mouth and I swelled further. Urgency colored my moves as I stumbled, still half wrapped around him, along the hallway and into the bedroom where we dropped onto the bed. Caleb fumbled with something on his bedside table. "Condom." Not wasting any time, he unwrapped it and rolled the lubricated condom on me, his touch drowning me in waves of pleasure. I wasn't going to last much longer.

"You know I love you, right?" *Shit.* It came out without warning. I was scared I may have ruined everything with my sentimental crap, but Caleb smiled at me. A smile that lit up the room and made me throb with yearning. He turned his back to me, my arm curving around his hips to touch him. His moan of pleasure was all the invitation I needed; I plunged inside him and we were one. It felt better than good. Being one with him was right, like Heaven. Better than Heaven. It was like finally being home.

In the aftermath of love, we lay together, my head on his shoulder, his hand playing with the loose curls of my hair. I couldn't resist exploring his body in a fluttering of fingers across his chest, his stomach. I noticed an ugly bruise stretching from one side of him to the other. When I touched it, he recoiled lightly. "Where did you get this?" Even though his body had been badly bruised in the accident, I was certain that one hadn't been there before. It looked almost like a burn, his skin blistered here and there along the bruise.

"It's nothing." Brushing it off wasn't going to work for me anymore. He was obviously in pain. I lifted my head and looked him in the eye. "The angels used something on me, not sure what it was."

I sat up, my hand on his stomach. "They tortured you, didn't they?" His eyes hid from mine. "Those sons of bitches. They'll pay for that." Even though I knew my angel

DNA would never allow me to actually be violent, I meant it. Maybe I wouldn't hurt them physically, but I would figure out a way of getting them back for what they'd done to Caleb. "Why didn't you tell me?"

"I didn't want to worry you or my sister." He sounded almost apologetic, as if the whole thing had been his fault. "It's nothing. It didn't last long. I'm just a little sore, that's all."

Turning on my side, I allowed my wings to stretch out. I curled my left leg over Caleb's and cocooned us in a cloud-like sheath with my wings. My lips pressed to his neck, I shuddered in sudden realization that his ordeal was far from over. It was all my fault. Drunk with love, I had precipitated a series of events that didn't bode well for Caleb or me. Only I wasn't worried about myself. *Que sera, sera.* It was what may happen to the man I loved that worried me sick.

"How come you never talk about it?" The question came from nowhere. I had thought about it, but why was I bringing it up right then of all times?

"Talk about what?" Caleb asked.

"The other angel you saw the day of your parents' accident." I regretted bringing it up as soon as it was out of my mouth. How insensitive of me to bring up such a delicate, painful memory. I was normally a lot more aware of emotional boundaries.

Caleb glanced over at me, a question in his eyes. "How did you know about the angel?"

I chuckled. "Your sister told me."

"Of course she did." He turned slightly to face me, still

sheltered underneath my wings. "I don't like to talk about it. In fact, I haven't ever talked about it with anyone. Not even my therapist."

My eyebrow shot up in question. "Therapist?" I couldn't imagine him needing therapy. I had never met anyone so put together like Caleb.

"Both Joan and I saw a therapist for a while after the accident. The authorities were worried we were traumatized." He slid his hand along my side. "But we weren't. Not the way they thought, at least."

I pulled him closer until his body was glued to mine. "You don't have to tell me if you don't want to."

He brushed his fingers on my face. "I want to. I don't talk about it not because it's painful—at least not the way people expect it to be. It's the guilt I feel when I think about it that bothers me."

"Guilt?" Why would he feel guilty? He wasn't at the wheel when the accident happened, and both he and Joan had been severely injured as well. I had read the file— studied it—and I knew no one had walked out of that accident unharmed.

"My rational side tells me it's stupid to feel guilty, but my heart has other ideas." He pressed his eyes shut for a second. "You know what's weird? I was asleep when it happened. I had gone partying with my friends the night before, so I fell asleep shortly after we left the house. You would think the impact and the pain of my injuries would've kept me unconscious, but it actually woke me up. I can't explain it, but suddenly there I was, scrunched up in the middle of a mangled car, my sister glued to my side and the lifeless bodies of my parents right in front of me." He swallowed, his Adam's apple bobbing up and down. "I knew it immediately. I knew they were dead."

My wings quivered a little as I pressed him tighter against me.

"Joan was also awake, whimpering against my side. She kept mumbling, calling my mom and dad, but I think she knew too. That's when the angel appeared, a being of light that managed to somehow spread his white wings inside that cramped space. Joan raised her hands to him, but he told her it wasn't her time. He was only taking my parents to a good, happy place. We watched him as he wavered and shimmered away, and we knew Mom and Dad were gone." In spite of the painful memories, Caleb was smiling.

"Why the guilt, then?"

"I feel guilty because I survived and they didn't. And I feel guilty for the strange sense of peace that came over me when the angel took their souls. Shouldn't I have felt sorrow or anger or any of those more appropriate feelings? Peace? Why would I feel peace?" His handsome face had contorted in pain, his mesmerizing eyes filled with tears.

I swiped a finger under his eye, collecting the wetness gathering there. "Caleb, you felt peace because you knew they were at peace. They weren't suffering and they were going to a wonderful place. That's why. Angels of light give off that vibe, that feeling. It's part of who we are. There's no shame in feeling that."

Caleb burrowed his face in the crook of my neck and

tightened his hold on me. "So glad you're here." His voice tickled my skin. "And glad I shared this with you. Thank you."

For a few moments we lay that way, entwined together in silence.

"So, is it true?" His voice was muffled against my neck and I didn't hear him at first. "Is it true?"

His skin against mine intoxicated me to the point that I was only slightly aware of my surroundings. "What are you talking about?"

"That you love me."

That sobered me up quickly. Not because it wasn't true or because I didn't want him to know. But I knew my overly sentimental heart sometimes messed things up for me. Oversharing of feelings so early in a relationship—did we even have that?—could be the straw that broke the camel's back, so to speak. Heavens knew Caleb had been dealing with way too many tough issues; the last thing he needed was to feel pressured by a clumsy, cheesy angel who couldn't keep his hands off him.

I looked up at him again. The rare gems he had for eyes shone in the dim room, expectant and—was I imagining it?—anxious.

"You told me you loved me," he repeated, his voice thick with emotion. "Do you? Or did you just say that because we were… well, you know."

My gulp sounded way too loud to my ears. I couldn't lie. Not to him. "I do. I've loved you since the first time I saw you." Caleb opened his mouth to say something but

I interrupted. "And don't say there's no such thing as love at first sight. I'm an angel. I dance to the beat of a different drum. I did fall in love with you as soon as I looked into your eyes."

Caleb smiled and my heart melted. Did he know the power he held over me every time he smiled like that? "You idiot!" Well, that was definitely not the response I expected. "Shut up and listen to me." He scooted away a little so he could more easily look me in the eye, though our legs were still tangled and my hand refused to leave his abs. "I love you too. Not sure why, but when you came to my door, it was as if we knew each other." I wanted to tell him we did know each other from before, but I couldn't. "I think you got me right then. One look and I was lost."

My heart must've grown a pair of wings, for it soared. I scooted up and melded my lips to his in a kiss I hoped showed all the feelings I had dancing around in my chest, overwhelming me with their intensity. Caleb may not remember me, but his heart surely did. That was more than enough for me.

✳✳✳

ALWAYS

Lucy stuffed her mouth with chocolate bonbons and tears rolled down my face. Beside me, Joan was folded in two, laughing so hard she ended up in a coughing fit. Joan had introduced me to *I Love Lucy*, and I couldn't believe I had lived as long as I had without ever watching one single episode of what had to be the funniest show ever.

The vibration in my pocket sobered me up. Gabriel!

Making an excuse, I walked out of the living room and into the small bathroom to talk in private. My hands shook as I slid my finger over the screen and brought it to my ear. "Hello?"

"Don't mention any names." Cryptic as always. Did it give him a sense of importance to make everything sound top secret? "Our dark friend is on the move again."

My sense of irritation turned into a ball inside my throat. "You couldn't have told me that before he took... the mortal?"

"I didn't find out about that until afterward." *Should I believe him?* It was still hard to swallow that the note I found on his desk wasn't really his, but he had let me go at great risk to his career. "This time I have better intel. He has something up his sleeve again." My stomach churned. The last thing I wanted to hear was that Caleb was in danger again. "Stick to the mortal like glue." That I wouldn't mind doing at all.

"I haven't been able to find out anything." The dreaded words were out. I actually clenched my eyes, waiting for the screaming that surely would ensue, but it never came. "It's very hard to work here without the resources I have up there. I'm pretty much working blind."

Gabriel was unusually quiet. When he spoke, his voice

was soft and cautious. "I know. Just keep an eye on the mortal and make sure nothing bad happens to him. I'll take care of the rest." And without any warning, he hung up on me.

Staring at the phone, I left the bathroom to join Joan on the couch. Caleb, sitting in my previous spot, raised his eyes to me and grinned. "Girlfriend called?"

"Jealous?" Laughing, I sat next to him, weaving my fingers between his. Joan looked between us and at our joined hands, her mouth agape. I bit my lip in amusement. "You're going to swallow a fly."

If at first muted by surprise, Joan quickly rediscovered her voice. "You guys got it on! When did this happen? Details, *mes amis*, I need details."

"Right! That's what we'll do, give you a step-by-step report." Caleb's voice dripped sarcasm, but it was obvious he was amused by his sister's shock. "It's none of your business, sis."

"Fuck! Well, I'm sure that's what you guys did—"

Caleb almost choked on his own tongue. "I told you before not to use that kind of language, girl!"

"Just because you're an old man trapped in the body of a twenty-eight-year-old doesn't mean I have to listen to you." Joan turned petulantly to me, ignoring the increasingly redder Caleb. "So how does that work in angel land? You guys have your straight angels and the gay ones? Are there girls as well?"

"Of all the stupid things to ask!" Caleb looked like he was about to have a stroke of sorts. It was endearing and funny to watch him react to his sister's irreverent personality.

A little chuckle escaped my lips, and I squeezed his hand. "It's okay. It's good to have a curious soul."

"Not if your curiosity is only for the most inappropriate issues." Stubborn, he didn't want to give in to his sister, but I could tell he wasn't angry at all.

"Angels are—well, angels. Yes, there are males and females, but there's no such thing as a straight or gay angelic creature. We were made to love, and love has no gender," I explained, my eyes seeking the soothing effect Caleb's had on me.

Joan seemed immersed in thought, so I took full advantage of the pause to rub my thumb on Caleb's palm, delighting in the smile I induced. "So technically you could have fallen in love with me instead of my brother," the elfin girl finally said, her eyebrow arched up high. "And I'd be the one with my hands all over that hot body of yours."

Caleb's hand went flying out of my grasp. "Holy shit, girl! You can be so freaking inappropriate." Joan was laughing, clearly enjoying the fact that she had rattled her brother. "If I didn't love you so much, I'd put you up for adoption."

"I'm practically an adult. I only stay with you because you need someone to take care of you." Not too far from the truth right then—not that Joan would have any power over the forces of evil, of course. She stuck her tongue out at him, the exact contrary of what she'd just claimed. "I'll leave the two lovebirds alone now. I have a possible boyfriend waiting for me at the mall." Grabbing her small purse from the table, she stood up and left the house, laughing.

Caleb stared at me, confused. "Did she say 'boyfriend'?"

Heavens, he was beautiful! I laid my hands on each side of his face and pulled it closer to mine. "Love it when you're cute like that."

Forgetting Joan for a moment, Caleb gave me one of his winning smiles. Slowly I touched my lips to his, suckling on the lower one before pulling it between my teeth. He shook, and parts of me melted while others went the opposite way.

"I knew it!" Joan's voice sounded from the door. She had sneaked back in. "As soon as I leave you alone, you're all over each other like rabbits in heat." She laughed, looking very satisfied that she'd caught us kissing. "Now that I made my point, I'll leave you to it." She had already turned around and was at the door when she looked back at us. "By the way, I'm so happy for the two of you. My favorite brother and my favorite angel together." With that, she left, closing the door behind her.

We both laughed, my hands still on his face. "You have a crazy woman for a sister."

"Don't I know it." We drank each other in with our eyes. "Why are you here, Sky? Really."

My stomach sank. Could I tell him without admitting everything? "To protect you from the dark angels. I'm not sure why, but they're after your soul. They caused your accident and they'll come back to finish it up. I'm here because I love you, and I won't let anything bad happen to you. Not if I can help it."

He was silent for a beat. "I believe you," he said, right

before kissing me.

I spent the rest of the day fussing over Caleb—and probably irritating the crap out of him—afraid to leave him even for a minute as Gabriel's words rang in my ears, dark and ominous. *What could Samael and his minions have in mind for my soul mate now? Will I be able to protect him when the time came? Or am I enough of a deterrent being by his side constantly?* I didn't think so. Samael looked far from put off when I walked in on him in the hospital room. He knew well that I was a nobody in angelic terms. Just an errand angel, really. The equivalent of a bike messenger— pick up souls, carry them to Heaven's door, start again. My job didn't require brains or even heart to some extent. The thought had occurred to me a few times throughout the years, but it hit me with a renewed strength at that point. The first thing I had ever done out of true love was rescuing Caleb, and look what I had started.

That night, after Joan went to bed, I wanted to ask Caleb if I could stay with him but couldn't find the courage to do it. I was afraid I would sound too clingy and scare him off. On the other hand, keeping an eye on him from the couch wasn't an easy task. I could, of course, work my magic and become invisible to him. I could sit in his bedroom all night, my eyes glued to his sleeping figure and my innards in a knot of frustrated wanting. I dismissed that option quickly. It wasn't right to trick someone you loved, someone you wanted to trust you.

While he was in the bathroom, I began spreading the sheets on the couch, my mind a mess of fears, frustrations, and percolating ideas that went nowhere fast. The sound of someone clearing his throat from behind brought me back to the here and now. I turned around to a shirtless Caleb, his pajama pants riding very low on his hips, revealing the V of his hip bones framing hard, well-defined abs. I gulped and involuntarily licked my lips. He didn't budge, his extraordinary eyes glued to mine, and I felt it again—that mental tug, soundless words calling me. I couldn't clearly understand them, but they beckoned me like his eyes. My feet moved then. I couldn't be sure I was the one making them move, but I was walking toward Caleb, who stood leaning against the doorway, intense and irresistible. He had magic in his eyes.

"You called?" The question escaped my lips in a whisper, and I wondered why I said it.

Caleb smiled, slowly tilting his head to the side. "Only in my thoughts. Can you hear them?"

I licked my lips again. "Only when you call me." In the back of my mind, I filed that information away, that tidbit of intel that may become valuable or useful in the future.

His laughter echoed in the quiet house. "Good. It would be creepy if you could read my thoughts." I had to agree with that. Not a superpower I was longing to have. Caleb looked behind me. "Why are you setting up the couch?"

I glanced behind me at the pile of pillows I had placed on the sofa. "Sorry. I thought you were going to bed. We can still sit and watch TV if you want." Part of me was relieved that he didn't seem to want to sleep yet. A good opportunity for me to keep guard easily.

As I turned back to him, I found myself staring directly into his face. Soundlessly, he had moved to stand just inches away from me, close enough for me to touch him. "What I mean is, why are you not staying in my room?"

Gasping for air, I could only nod. I wanted to stay with him. Not just for the night, and not because he needed my protection, but because without him, I was as incomplete as if I were missing a leg—or, more accurately, my heart. I craved his presence like some people craved caffeine or drugs. My life up to the moment I met him on that beach had lost all meaning. For him, I would give up my wings.

"Don't you get it, Sky?" He took another step closer and lifted one hand to the side of my neck, my skin immediately reacting to it as if touched by electricity. The tingling started under his palm and moved fluidly through my body all the way to my extremities. "I want you with me. Always."

If I weren't an angel already, I would've thought I'd died and gone to Heaven.

PAIN

ASMY

"You work?" My surprise seemed slightly out of place. How could he maintain a house and make plans to put his sister through college if he didn't have a job? Only it had never been mentioned before. So busy and wrapped up in everything that had happened—good and bad—we had never talked about his professional life.

Caleb chuckled. "No, I'm really a billionaire living off my fortune. Of course I work. I've just been a little under the weather for the last couple months." He scratched his day-old stubble. "I'm officially out of excuses not to go back."

"Caleb is a bigwig at a local magazine." Joan was by the refrigerator, the door wide open and her head almost totally inside the appliance.

"No, I'm not." I helped him look for his keys which had gone missing. I suspected Joan as the culprit; she seemed even less enthusiastic about her brother leaving the safety of the house for the wide-open world outside. "I'm a man of all trades. My official title is editor, but I also manage web content and other odd jobs. It's a small magazine." He straightened and looked around. "Where the hell are my keys?"

Joan closed the fridge door. "Don't look at me! I have no idea. If you ever find them, we need milk." She walked by me and winked. Hell, she knew where the keys were.

"Maybe you should ask for a few more days off," I suggested hopefully. "You had brain surgery, after all. I think they would understand."

He sighed. "They'll let me work from home, I'm sure, but I need to talk to them about it." Turning around, he picked up a few cushions to check underneath them. "Damn keys."

"Can I go with you?" I bit my tongue. *Could I sound any needier?* "I'm here to protect you, remember?"

Caleb kissed me lightly. "Sure, come with me. I want you to meet my boss."

I rolled my eyes like a teenager. "Hope he's better than mine." Gabriel may have let me go, but he was still far from my favorite angel.

After giving up on finding the missing keys, he decided to leave the door unlocked and we left with Joan in tow, her school on the way. "I much prefer you guys' company— even if you are a couple of horrible old prudes—to my so-called BFF who can't talk of anything else but this idiot she met at a party last weekend." She made a gagging sound. "My stomach can't handle it anymore."

Wiscasset is a beautiful little town where you always

seem to either be going up or down. The only flat area was the waterfront. As we descended Bath Road, the main street, we stopped for a cup of coffee in a local bakery and then continued leisurely all the way down to where we said goodbye to Joan. The harbor was quiet at that time of morning, the waters still covered in a light mist, reminding me of the cloud layer between Arcadia and Earth. Suddenly nostalgic, I had a desire to share my world with Caleb as he'd shared his with me. But I couldn't. Our worlds were so far apart, I might as well be from another planet. The weight of the realization hit my chest. Was our relationship doomed to fail?

"Why the face?" Caleb laid his arm across my shoulders and gave me a gentle tug. "The sun is shining—well, trying to shine through the clouds. I'm healthy and alive, Joan is off to school, and you're here. What's to be sad about?"

I managed a tiny smile. "Just worried about what's yet to come." *And what may never happen. Like our happy-ever-after.*

Caleb let go and walked a few steps backward, facing me. That melt-your-heart smile was back on his face as he stuffed his hands inside the pockets of his hoodie. The air had that chilly tang announcing the impending winter. "Why worry about what you can't change? Instead, why don't we just enjoy this time together? Be thankful that we found each other and I didn't die in that freaky accident."

I cringed a little at his words. If he only knew.

With a shake of my head, I allowed my lips to stretch fully into a smile. He was right. We were together. He was alive and well. We loved each other. I had a new appreciation for love, the kind that came attached to no strings, no demands. The kind that made you invincible and gave you wings— even when you'd had them all your life. I threaded my arm through the loop of his and walked beside him.

We were in no hurry, so our walk along the waterfront stretched for a couple of miles. As we were about to turn around and go back, a heaviness formed in my chest as if an elephant had sat on it. Had I not been an angel, I would've thought I was having a heart attack, but I knew, as certain as I was of the wings starting to twitch on my back, that we were in danger.

A black, thick, and slimy wave of evil covered my thoughts and senses in a layer of tar-like material, flexible but impervious and opaque. Samael was using mind control on me. I didn't even know a common angel could use that power on another angelic being, but I sure recognized the signs. Soon, I would be too confused to tell what was going on around me.

I held on to Caleb for dear life. "What's wrong, Sky?" I could still hear his voice, but I couldn't see him anymore, blackness overcoming me. "Are you all right? Sky?"

Somehow I was aware of my hold on his arm, terrified as I was of losing him, of letting him go. "He's coming," I managed to say—at least, I think I did. The descending darkness was almost complete and I slid down to the ground, my legs buckling underneath my weight, a fading sense of awareness in the back of my mind.

Stars sprinkled the inside of my eyelids and the day

began to slowly dawn. Only it wasn't the morning light that began seeping through my daze. Instead, a sickly reddish gloom surrounded me and everything in sight. Strangely, I was standing up—no, floating. A weird sense of pull made me look at my hands. Straps attached to the ceiling—was there even a ceiling? I couldn't see all the way to the top— tightly held my wrists. I glanced at my feet and realized my ankles were also bound by glowing straps, holding me spread eagle slightly over the floor.

I studied the straps—seraphic rope. I could wiggle, stretch, and pull, but those knots weren't going anywhere. No force on Earth or in Heaven could break the straps.

The fuzz in my brain cleared slowly but steadily, and I could finally try to make some sense of the situation. Why had Samael taken me instead of Caleb? Or did he? Maybe he had taken both of us. I twisted around, looking for signs of my soul mate, but couldn't find any.

A roll of deep laughter reached my ears from the dark, invisible corners of the room, followed by a slow, mocking applause. "Don't bother looking for your mortal. He's not here."

Samael emerged from the shadows, a creature of darkness himself. His jet-black wings arrogantly unfolded behind him, his black eyes intent on me, hungry and rabid. He stopped clapping and came to stand, legs apart, next to me.

"What do you want from me?" I scanned the room, desperately looking for something, anything that would give me the hope of escape. Samael's eyes followed my every move, like a predator stalking his prey.

"Just a bit of fun. Even dark angels like to amuse themselves a bit once in a while." I dared not ask what he meant by "a bit of fun." I knew it wouldn't be something I cared for. "You, on the other hand, have been having all kinds of fun on Earth with your delicious little mortal. You have been a serious pain in my ass, constantly getting in my way. Aren't angels of light supposed to be unselfish and unobtrusive? Why can't you just stay out of my business?"

My stomach rumbled and I tasted bile for the first time in my life. Not many things scared me, but Samael absolutely terrified me with his viscous, slithering voice and lazy, penetrating eyes. And he was after Caleb.

"I figured I would teach you a lesson." The dark angel paced around me slowly, his hands behind his back, wings haughtily fanned behind him. "So, sweet angel of death, I will make you squirm a bit—just as a reminder of how much I hate your interference, you understand. Once I tire of hurting you, I'll double the fun by doing the same with your mortal."

The scream came out before I could stop it. I could handle whatever this creature of darkness threw at me, but I couldn't handle it done to Caleb. Just the idea of him in the hands of this monster made me quake in horror. "Where is he? What have you done to him?"

Samael made a mocking frown of concern. "Sweet little angel, don't worry so much. He's safe—or is he? I guess you'll find out eventually." He stopped right in front of me, poked me in the belly with a finger, and licked his lips obscenely. "In the meantime, you go first, my sweet one."

I closed my eyes and uttered a prayer. Whatever he was planning to do to me, I could take it, but that didn't mean it wouldn't be excruciatingly unpleasant. I wouldn't give him the pleasure of seeing me tremble though. "Bring it on, Samael." I hoped the bravado in my voice was a lot more convincing that what I felt inside.

A wave of his hand and I flipped over, my head just off the floor and my ankles burning from the pull of the angelic rope. Blood surged to my head, but I was used to it from my crazy plunges to Earth. What worried me was what I saw materialize in his hands—a black whip sword that glittered in the dim light of the room, betraying the sharp shards of seraphic crystal that edged its blade. In spite of my resolve, my body trembled and my stomach churned.

"I see you are acquainted with my friend here." He caressed the whip sword as if patting a beloved pet, and the damned thing seemed to shimmer in delight. My eyes had to be playing tricks on me. "Oh, don't make the mistake of thinking the blood rushing to your head is making you hallucinate. My wicked Asmy here is very much alive, blessed into being by its namesake."

He paced around me one more time, and I couldn't help but shiver in apprehension every time I lost visual track of him. My wrists and ankles were bound so tightly I couldn't move even an inch, and my stretched body, covered only in a thin pair of what looked like black pajama pants, was beginning to ache.

"Asmodeus, my lord and master, gifted me this whip sword as a reward for having served him well. My sweetie here has a black heart like mine and enjoys much of the same sport as I do." Fear, an unusual feeling for me, was rising in my gut and climbing up to my throat. "And neither of us likes it when some fucker gets in our way."

Samael came to a stop in front of me. My upside-down position had one advantage: everything, including the dark angel, seemed less real. It gave me the courage to forget my growing panic and pretend I couldn't care less what happened to me. "Stop yakking away already, Samael!" My voice came out tainted with a weariness I didn't feel but was hoping to project. "Whatever you have planned for me, do it already! I'm getting bored."

I was rewarded with a cringe of surprise and annoyance. Samael was expecting groveling and fear; I was ruining his fun. On the negative side, I had just irritated the one person who could do me serious injury.

I swallowed my fear and accepted my fate. This was going to hurt.

***

THE BURNING

The first strike came, and I didn't know what to expect. The whip sword had stretched and unrolled from its pommel like a lethal ribbon and slithered in the air, its crystal-shard teeth catching and reflecting flickers of light as it moved. I closed my eyes, as if by doing so I could stop it from striking my helpless body. It didn't. The sharp teeth dug their way through the skin of my belly and chest as the weapon wrapped around me and buried its tip on my back. A scream of pain escaped my lips and I hated myself for it. So when Samael, with a flip of his hand, pulled the whip sword from me, chunks of my flesh flying away with it, I bit my tongue hard enough to draw blood but didn't scream again.

The second blow came shortly after, the wicked whip sword's tongue cutting deep into my legs and thighs. Amidst the agonizing pain, I was aware of the warm stream of blood that oozed from my many different wounds. I wished I could pass out, yearning as I was for oblivion, but angels didn't react the same to the loss of blood. It would take a lot more abuse before my brain finally gave up and went blank, and Samael knew that. For him, it must've been a lot more entertaining to torture an angel than a human. We lasted longer. The fun was over when the victim either fainted or died, but the dark angel knew he could torment me for a very long time.

I wasn't sure how long the torture lasted. After the first handful of attacks, my mind—although conscious of every cut and tear of skin and muscle—went numb. In the past, I had heard humans describe a near-death experience like that. My consciousness seemed to have separated from my body and it hovered above, watching, sympathizing but distant.

I watched in morbid fascination as the whip sword came down on me again and again, each time loosening a shower of blood and torn flesh into the air. The gruesome storm fell upon the dark angel, covering his face and bare arms, turning his skin a sickly red hue. Samael cackled like an old witch in near ecstasy and licked the blood drops that fell near his lips, his tongue flickering out of his mouth like that of a snake, his eyelids shuttering in pleasure.

When I least expected it, the torture stopped. From under my bloodied eyelids, I watched the evil angel as he retracted the dripping whip sword into its pommel, sheathed it behind his back, and wiped his hand on his own pants. "Don't you worry, sweet angel of light. I will come back. I grow tired of this game. Need a change." He walked slowly toward one of the dark corners of the room. "It'll give you some time to regenerate so we can have even more fun later."

The heaviness in my eyelids began to force them to close. As much as I didn't want to sleep or even regenerate, there was nothing I could do to stop the natural instincts of my savaged body. When he came back, I'd have healed enough to go another long round of abuse.

Before he was engulfed in the shadows, Samael turned around one last time. "Oh, and I'll check on your lover while I'm at it. I want to make sure he's safe and sound for the plucking later."

My eyes popped open and I fought against my restraints with all the strength I had left. "Leave him alone. You got me. What do you need him for?"

Samael's wicked laughter echoed through the room.

"You're fucking funny. I see why the human finds you so attractive. The more pain inflicted, the better. Watching you squirm while I do to him what I did to you will be the cherry on top." To better illustrate what he meant, the dark angel swiped his obscene tongue across his lips. "Can't wait."

Left hanging upside down, I cried. What started as whimpering quickly turned to uncontrollable sobbing. My eyes, scratched and bleeding, burned with the saltiness of the tears that erupted so unexpectedly. My chest hurt every time a sob made it spasm and quake. My tears fell for what was coming, for the horrors Caleb would have to endure while I hung there helplessly. It was all my fault. Out of selfishness, I had triggered a chain of events that I now stood powerless against. Love had blinded me to everything else, and now Caleb and his soul were in terrible danger.

When Samael came back, I had exhausted my tears. My numbness was gone, and even though my body was beginning to quickly regenerate, pain was back in force. There wasn't a single inch of my body that didn't hurt. The bleeding had largely stopped, but the throbbing pain had grown and shattered my whole being. It was hard to breathe, for even the normal inhale and exhale movements made my chest burn.

"Back so soon?" Fighting the debilitating pain, I goaded him. I hoped to distract him from his ultimate goal— bringing Caleb to this hellhole.

Samael scowled at me. "You're in for a special treat." His tone stung me like a needle. "I had an interesting conversation with Asmodeus, and he had a great idea."

Asmodeus's great ideas often caused great destruction and pain. Whatever he had come up with to further torment me would certainly count as a treat only for the likes of Samael. I had very little fight left, for all the good it did me. I couldn't move, couldn't do a thing about it.

"So, my lord and master reminded me of angelic fire." The one thing capable of destroying angels with one strike. I twitched. *Is he finally going to kill me?* "I always think of it as the ultimate weapon against annoying angels. Good to get rid of the heavenly vermin. But angel fire has another function. Granted, it isn't used very often and is frowned upon even by the dark angels, but desperate times call for desperate measures."

He had lost me. I couldn't think of any other thing angelic fire was good for other than killing seraphic creatures.

The dark angel started pacing again, stopping every once in a while to touch my wounds—sometimes gently, almost tenderly, other times to shove a finger in the open wound and twist. It seemed as if it were some routine he followed often, maybe something he thought he had to do to calm himself or assure himself he was still in control.

"Unfurl your wings, angel!" The order was so unexpected I almost jumped out of my skin. He waved his hand in the air and I started moving, spinning to a standing position. My head was heavy and my sight wavered from being upside down for so long. "I want to see your beautiful, white wings."

Like hell he did. *What's he plotting?*

When I didn't comply, Samael took a few steps closer

to me and, flapping his own wings, floated up until his face was right in front of mine. "Unfurl. Your. Wings." Spittle flew out of his mouth and hit me in the face. My stomach churned in disgust. "If you don't do it on your own, I have interesting ways of doing it for you. But I can't promise you'll like it."

Not convinced, I spread out my wings anyway. Why give him reason to hurt me further? My feathers burst up from my back as a cloud of white smoke, in stark contrast with the dark environment. In spite of my situation, it felt wonderful. A sense of freedom, even in my magic shackles, invaded my spirit as peace replaced the fear and pain. At least for a moment.

Samael's face contorted into what passed for a smile in his world, and I saw a glint of satisfaction in his eyes. I didn't like it. "That wasn't so hard, now was it?" With a flick of his hands, a frightening, sparkling sample of angelic fire appeared. He flew behind me and panic rose in my heart. I heard him move back and forth as if stalking me. "Oh, this is going to be beautiful."

The pain defied explanation or definition. A tang of burnt feathers reached my nostrils and hit me with the force of a fist. I tried to turn around and look behind me, but I couldn't move. The pain spread from the tips of my wings to their roots on my back, like a wave of locusts eating through my beloved feathers.

What's happening?

"Asmodeus pointed out that angelic fire will burn an angel's wings forever. It'll destroy your power of regeneration for good." *No, not that. Not my wings.* "I'm afraid, my sweet angel, that you'll never fly again."

Angel feathers don't burn like birds'. They burn slow and hot, infusing the air with the stench of burning flesh. I threw my head back in despair and watched helplessly as the ashes of my wings floated into the air, spiraling up to the darkness above. I could hear crackling as the fire devoured my most precious of possessions, one feather at a time.

Pain and sorrow deafened me to the sound of Samael's mocking laughter. The dark angel had circled back to face me, watching as what defined me went up in flames. I wanted to be able to hate with the same intensity with which I was capable of loving, but I couldn't. Sadness took over instead. In agony, I mourned for my blazing wings, my scorched heart beating to the sound of unspeakable grief.

When my wings were nothing more than smoldering ambers burning the skin of my back, I heard it. It was faint at first, the sound of agitated voices at a distance, but even from beneath the pain-induced daze, I could hear them coming closer. Samael heard them too, his laughter dying on his lips and his eyes suddenly focused on the shadows behind him.

A banging noise immediately followed by yelling erupted behind the dark angel, and I was conscious enough to notice him cringe—was it surprise or fear? "Bring him down. Now!" The male voice echoed in the room.

Gabriel? Could it be, or am I hallucinating?

Two figures came through the darkness, and I strained my aching eyes to see who they were.

My heart jumped to my throat. *Caleb! No, leave now while you can.* Right beside him, Gabriel, all seven feet of him, waved a hand above his head and my restraints relaxed as I was brought down to the ground finally. My numb legs couldn't hold me, but as I dropped to my knees, Caleb was there to soften the fall. He shimmied out of his jacket and used it to snuff out what was left of the flames at my back.

"My God, Sky. Your wings." Caleb's voice, even panicked, was a balm for my soul. "What did they do to you?"

I lifted a bloodstained hand and blindly sought his. He met me halfway and held on for dear life. "Caleb, you're in danger. Leave now." I wanted him to be there and also to be gone, away to safety, away from that monster.

I felt the softness of his lips on my knuckles. "It's okay. Gabriel is taking care of things. We're safe now." I knew I was dreaming. A hallucination induced by the pain and fear overwhelming my heart and soul. But I so wanted it to be true.

For the second time that day, I cried. Bitter tears of sorrow for the wings I had lost and for the love I would surely lose should Samael have anything to say about it.

WINGLESS
ASHES

Curled up like a child in a mother's womb, I remained motionless for who knew how long. Caleb and Gabriel had taken me home, where an inconsolable Joan joined her brother to nurse me the best she could, cleaning wounds yet to regenerate, cooing and comforting all the while. I felt I should get up and rejoice in the fact that I was back with the ones I loved, but my grief held me captive as tightly as those angelic straps had earlier. I had lost my wings, my freedom, my joy… my soul. Voiceless and lifeless, I lay curled up in bed, my knees bent all the way to my chest, eyes open but unseeing.

Sometime later, Caleb sat next to me, a cup of steaming tea in his hand. "Lavender. Your favorite." His quiet yet powerful voice snapped me out of my trance, and I glanced at him. My beautiful human. Caleb's dark, short hair stuck up a little as if he hadn't combed it yet, and his face was covered in a thicker than usual stubble. His soothing lavender field eyes were rimmed in red.

Although my muscles hurt from being immobile for so long, I reached out to touch his face. "Thank you."

He set the teacup on the table and, bending down, gingerly kissed me. "Don't want to hurt you. You have so many wounds." At the warmth of his breath on my lips, my heart filled with love again. Gradually, as his lips pried mine open and his tongue caressed the inside of my mouth, life returned to my body, ran through my veins, rejuvenating and restoring my faith in all that was good.

Little by little, I stretched my legs and pulled him down beside me with my aching arms. I hadn't lost my soul. Not completely. Flying had always been the one thing that made me happy, but there was something else now.

Someone.

"I was so scared, Caleb."

His eyes were suspiciously shiny. I brushed my hand across the stubble on his face, rejoicing in the familiar scratch against my skin.

"I know you were. Who wouldn't be?" He scanned my face and gently touched the bruises and cuts that peppered my face, now beginning to heal.

"I was scared for you." It still burned in my heart, the paralyzing fear that Samael would get his filthy, cruel hands on my love. "Samael is evil, and he was determined to have his fun at your cost. I couldn't bear it, Caleb."

His arms went around and beneath me, his face flattened against my chest. I could feel my heart pounding against his skin in a love song. "We're okay. We're going to be all right."

When morning came, we hadn't budged an inch. I had slept. Really slept all night in the arms of my personal angel. I had been sent to Earth to harvest his soul, but he had saved me in more ways than one. As I opened my eyes, blinking against the intruding sunlight peeking through the curtains, I noticed Joan standing by the bed, eyes swollen from crying, wringing her hands and watching her brother and me sleeping.

"Good morning, Joan." Careful not to wake Caleb, I waved her closer. "Come join us. I think we all need a great big group hug." She didn't need a second invitation. The elfin girl climbed onto the bed and stretched herself behind me, holding her brother on the other side of me. I could hear her tiny sobs and feel the moisture of her tears on my neck. We lay quiet for a while, allowing the heat between the three of us to recharge and console us.

After a while, she stopped crying. "I feel like the ham in a great big sandwich." I wanted to make her laugh again, to hear that young, crystalline giggling of hers. She didn't disappoint.

"What makes you think you'd be a ham? You have quite an inflated opinion of your looks, don't you?" She let go of us and sat on the edge of the bed, still behind me. Reluctantly, I also released the sleeping Caleb and turned on my back so I could see her. "You'd be more like turkey, I think. What with all those feathers—" She stopped herself and looked positively horrified. "Oh my God! I can't believe I just said that after you lost—"

I sat up and held her hands in mine. "Honey, it's okay.

You can make jokes." I needed her silly and snotty jokes right then. I needed to feel lighter and brighter and forget all the terrible things that had happened. "I love your jokes. Well, most of them." With a smile, I gave her hands a tug, encouraging her to go on. Her face relaxed and her smile came back.

"I'm so sorry about your beautiful wings, Sky." She scooted closer to me. "I hope that idiot dark angel gets what he deserves."

"Nothing will happen to him. Being cruel is his job." It was a fact, pure and simple. Yes, Samael was more brutal than most, but that was the one thing that made him Asmodeus's favorite. I was suddenly reminded that I didn't know exactly what had happened. How had Gabriel and Caleb ended up in that hellish place? How had they been able to stop Samael? I asked Joan.

"When that fucking winged idiot took you, he left something behind." Joan threw a glance at her brother to make sure he hadn't heard her cursing. He stirred and she paused, as if expecting him to rebuke her. He tossed a little and turned to the other side. "Caleb says the dark angel picked you up by your feet and your phone fell from your pocket. He knew Gabriel calls you on that phone sometimes, so he looked up the caller ID and gave him a ring."

Caleb stirred again. He was slowly waking up, his eyes fluttering and his nose twitching.

"Caleb called Gabriel?" I didn't even know it was possible for a mortal to call an angel.

My beloved had turned around and was now staring at

the two of us with an amused smile on his face. "Yes, I called Gabriel, and you were right—he's an asshole." I laughed at his conclusion. "But nevertheless, he didn't want one of his angels—even you—to suffer at the hands of the dark ones, so he pulled some strings, called a few head angels, and was able to get special permission to go to Hellgates and get you."

I was impressed that he had learned so much about my world in such a short time. "That was actually Abaddon," I corrected him. "Hellgates is further out. Once you're in, there's very little chance you'll ever get out."

The pointed glare I received for my troubles shut me down. "Gabriel said your body will regenerate a bit slower than usual because of the angel fire, but you'll still heal much faster than a human. He wants you to call him as soon as you're well enough. Something about an investigation."

What about Caleb? Is he safe now, or is his soul still up for grabs? What's going to happen to him now? What's going to happen to me? A lifetime of desk work away from the one I love? So many questions cluttered my brain. I shook my head and endeavored to focus on the most important thing right then. *Whatever may happen in the future, I have Caleb and Joan with me now. It would be stupid to waste such an opportunity.*

"What did he say about my wings?" I had to ask, even though I knew the painful answer. I had never once met an angel without wings. Ever.

Silence dropped and enveloped us all. Joan stood up. "I'll leave the two of you to talk about it. I'll be baking cookies if you need me. We desperately need sugar right now. Lots of it." She left the room and it was silent again.

"They won't regenerate, Sky." Like a double-edged blade, hearing what I already knew was true pierced me through my soul. "Gabriel said the Department of Wings will be working on creating a prosthetic for you, so you can eventually fly again, but you'll never regrow your own." If the expression on my face reflected my misery, it must've been hard to see. Caleb's own face contorted in pain. "I'm so sorry, Sky. I know what those wings meant to you."

I spoke then out of a need to share my pain with him, to share all of me with him. "It's like someone yanked a piece of my still-beating heart from my chest and set it on fire. My wings were more than a limb. They were my soul, my freedom. When I flew down to Earth, the wind on my face and my feathers flapping soundlessly, I was happy. So very happy."

Hesitantly at first, Caleb moved closer. "I know." He lowered his voice to a mere whisper and, getting on his knees, he crawled around until he kneeled behind me. He touched the now-empty roots of my wings with warmth and tenderness. "I would give anything to bring back your wings, but I can't." He caressed and massaged the raw wounds, sending shivers of comfort through the sensitive skin already growing over them. "I loved your wings too, but I'm just happy you're alive and well. I don't love you any less because you can't fly anymore." He pressed his warm lips against my neck and I trembled against them.

"You are part of my soul now, Caleb." I turned around to

face him, my muscles groaning at the movement. "As much as I loved my wings, you are now the one thing that makes me happy. The one person I don't ever want to lose. I love you." Like the first time I met him, I tilted his chin up with my finger and kissed him. "This kiss is what I long for now. You are my wings."

****

CLUELESS

Gabriel was his usual taciturn self as he sat across from me at the kitchen table, distractedly munching on Joan's cookies and staring at me.

"You're feeling better, right?" My boss didn't do sensitive well. I considered asking him about his date, but I bit my tongue and smiled instead. "We still need to find out who in headquarters is making deals with the devil." Quite literally, as it turned out.

"I'm a little limited in my movements right now." I wasn't sure he caught the sarcasm in my voice. "But I'll do what I can. What about Caleb?"

Gabriel frowned, a quizzical expression on his handsome face. "What about him?"

Gabriel might've been obtuse and annoying, but he was probably the only one who could help us. "Is Samael still after him?"

"Samael has been taken care of. He won't be bothering you or Caleb anymore." *That's it? No more details?* "You're still in charge of his soul keeping. However you choose to do that is up to you."

Did I hear a note of sarcasm in his voice? Is Gabriel even capable?

"Not sure how I can help with the resources I have here, Gabriel." It had to be said. I was at a total loss on how to proceed with any kind of investigation if I couldn't even fly. What I was supposed to investigate was all the way in Arcadia.

"I'll send you some documents for you to study, and I'm giving you the privilege to access the headquarters directory. Feel free to contact any angel you like and ask whatever questions you feel like asking."

Gabriel looked like he had just tasted something foul. I was enjoying seeing him squirm. Asking me for any favors had to be as distasteful to him as sucking on dog feces. "Just please be careful what you say to certain individuals. I can't keep you safe forever if you insist on ruffling everyone's feathers. Watch your mouth, you hear?"

I nodded, knowing all too well that I'd be more than happy to ruffle as many feathers as I could in order to find out who had gotten me and Caleb in this mess. Being unable to hate didn't prevent me from wanting some kind of retribution and closure. Especially closure. I longed for the day when I could walk away from Caleb without fear of never seeing him again. In spite of Gabriel's assurances, I knew as long as whoever signed that contract with Samael and his minions was out there, Caleb would never be totally safe.

"I have to go back," he said, standing up while picking up another chocolate chip cookie. "This girl is an amazing baker!" He took another bite. "And Sky, we're working on your prosthetic wings. I'm sorry I didn't get to you soon enough. No angel deserves having his wings burned like that." For once, Gabriel sounded sincere.

I thanked him, and he was gone.

Joan walked in and stared at the almost empty cookie platter. "Who ate all the cookies?" I gestured up to the sky. "Fucking archangel! He could've left some for us."

"Will you please stop using that language?" Caleb was right behind her, scowling. "Did Gabriel say anything interesting?"

I rolled my eyes. "That'll be the day." I laughed, hooking my arm around Joan's neck. "Are you going to bake more cookies, squirt? Gabriel is a big fan." She groaned and wiggled away from me. "What? You don't like my angel hugs?"

Throwing her arms up in the air, she walked away from us and into the living room, cursing under her breath.

Caleb watched me from under half-closed eyelids. The muscles of his crossed arms bulged from the short sleeves of a T-shirt that stretched tight across his chest. My body immediately responded to him. The thin joggers I was wearing apparently made it pretty obvious, his lips lifting at the corner.

"Don't be so cocky. I happen to find Gabriel very sexy."

I laughed at my own joke, strolling toward him.

"Oh really?" Caleb straightened and stepped forward until our bodies were touching. Unhurriedly, he ran a hand from my neck to the waist of my pants and then lower still. I moaned and pressed myself against him. "So who's hotter? Gabriel or me?"

I was just about to show him how hot I thought he was when Joan came barreling through the door. "Oh my God! I did not need to see that." She covered her eyes and shuffled inside the kitchen. Caleb and I quickly pulled apart, my hands automatically covering my arousal. I heard Caleb snicker behind me as a wave of heat turned me scarlet from head to toe. "I cannot unsee what I just saw. What the hell, can't you guys use the bedroom?"

My heavenly body had regenerated almost completely. A couple of deeper wounds were taking longer to heal, but all in all, the two weeks that had passed since my kidnapping had done their job.

On the other hand, my burnt wings still haunted me. Like humans who had lost a limb, I had frequent phantom pains. I would catch myself reaching for my wings or trying to unfurl them, and every time reality hit me with the power of a bulldozer. My heart shrank and my hands trembled. I didn't regret having saved Caleb and risking everything for him—he was my love, my heart, and my soul—but my wings were as much a part of me as any other vital organ, a part that defined me, gave my life purpose. Nightmares still troubled my sleep, and it wasn't uncommon for me to wake up suddenly drenched in sweat, the wing roots on my back burning as intensely as they had that fateful day. Caleb would patiently draw me to him, cradle me in his arms, and hold me until my body stopped shaking and the tears stopped falling. His love lifted me in the same way my wings used to.

Joan left for the library—or so she claimed. I suspected there was a new boy in the picture, and this sudden fever for knowledge had more to do with hormones than intellect. Caleb seemed oblivious to it, so I let it go; love had saved me, so why would I begrudge her the same joy?

That said, I had followed her out onto the porch and slipped a condom in her bag. "Just in case. Look at it as a lifesaver." She had laughed, stuck her tongue out at me, and called me "fucking weird" before running down the hilly street. That girl had a seriously filthy mouth.

Caleb was inside, sitting at the computer and looking positively sexy with his reading glasses hanging on the tip of his perfect nose, his disheveled hair, and bare feet. I tiptoed behind and enveloped him in my arms, my head resting on the crook of his neck. "What are you doing?"

"Working. I have a story due by tomorrow." He turned his head toward mine and planted a quick kiss on my lips. I flattened my hands on his chest, feeling the hard muscle beneath the cotton material. "I've been idle too long. Angels may not need money, but we lowly mortals have to work for a living."

"I work!" Feigning outrage at his insinuation, I nibbled on his earlobe. He quivered, and satisfaction filled me. "Well, I did until recently. But if I'm bothering you, I'll leave you be." I made as to leave, but he grabbed my arms, and in a smooth and quick move, he had me sitting on his lap.

"You are the worst tease. Are all angels like that?" He buried his face in my neck, nuzzling me gently. "God, you smell good." Beneath me I felt him swell, and shivers jolted through my body. This human had magic in him. "Shit, Sky. Now you got me all hot and bothered." He groaned and slipped a hand inside my pants, curving it around my backside in a caress.

There was not a lot of work done for the next hour or so, but eventually both of us had to get back to real life. Caleb returned to his laptop, and I retreated to our room to do the same. I figured as long as I could physically see him I would never get anything done.

Joan's laptop seemed to be staring at me as if mocking my lack of ideas as to how to proceed with this investigation. I had no clue where to start. With everything that had happened the last few weeks, I hadn't had much time to think about it. Now I sat there, my hands on my lap, looking at the empty screen and muttering a quiet prayer. "God, I've always served you to the best of my capacity. Please help me find out who's after Caleb. I'll do whatever you ask of me."

The screen flickered and lit up, much to my surprise. Across it, words began to form.

Who was in a position to place that note on Gabriel's desk?

Well, Gabriel for one, but I was sure he had nothing to

do with it. He may be an asshole, but he wasn't evil. So, who else had easy access to his office when he wasn't there? In spite of his open-door policy, we all knew not to enter his space when he was away from his desk. Whoever put that note there had to have gone in while he was away.

Think, angel, think. It all seemed like a lifetime ago, buried in the twilight of the past. Gabriel had left his office minutes before I went in at his request. Headquarters had been pretty empty; most angels had gone home already, I remembered. What was I missing? Someone must've been lurking around, but I couldn't think of anyone.

Desperate, I pulled up the directory Gabriel had so kindly—or out of guilt, most likely—given me access to.

The screen filled with names and faces of every angel who worked at headquarters. I filtered the information by departments, isolating it to the main lobby, where I worked, and the boss's floor. As I scrolled down the list, I grew disheartened. I couldn't recall any of them being around at that time. It was a long list, organized alphabetically.

Toward the end of the list, Cranky Amy's name appeared. Amy Zephyr. I chuckled quietly. *Zephyr, indeed.* The name meant "a gentle breeze," which was ironic considering there was nothing gentle about her. The breeze part I could understand since she was full of hot air most of the time.

Wait! Wasn't Amy in the office when I left that day? I closed my eyes, trying to remember. *Was she there? I remember thinking it was weird that she was gone earlier than usual. Shit, I don't know.* My brain just hadn't been the same since Samael and his not-so-tender ministrations.

Swiss cheese seemed to have replaced a great part of my memory of late. Gabriel claimed it was the side effects of angel fire, much like chemo on humans. "It's temporary, Sky. Don't worry." I hoped he was right.

I shook my head and buried my face in my arms crossed over the keyboard. Hell, was she there or not? The computer pinged, and I snapped my head up. On the screen there was a picture of a video camera. "Are you trying to tell me something, Father?"

Of course, the video monitors! Headquarters didn't have much need of video surveillance, but there was a camera pointed at the main entrance for security purposes. Legend had it that a few disgruntled fallen angels had once tried to besiege headquarters in protest of their condemnation. I was of the opinion that the camera was there so Gabriel could "escape" when someone he didn't want to talk to walked in.

Typing away like a secretary on crack, I pulled up the recordings for that day and fast-forwarded them to just before Gabriel left the office. I watched as the archangel came to tell me to make the call to Michael, then left. For the next ten minutes or so, there was nothing happening while I went upstairs to Gabriel's office, but suddenly I saw her, Cranky Amy, entering the room from a back office and crossing ways with me on my way out. She was there after all! And she had free access to Gabriel's office.

Could she be the one? What motivation could she have for doing something like that? Amy had never liked me very much, but neither did a lot of other angels. Not a strong enough motive to make a pact with the dark side. For once

I wished I had been a little more observant of those around me at work; I lived in my own little bubble, and that wasn't helping me much right now. I closed my eyes and went through a million memories. Not the important ones, for something told me the heart of the problem was probably something I dismissed as banal or negligible.

The door cracked open and Caleb's handsome face peeked through. "Fancy a break?"

Do I ever! "What exactly do you have in mind?" My eyebrow arched all the way up, and I tilted my head while scanning him from head to toe.

Caleb laughed and shook his head. "You have a dirty mind, sweet angel. I meant going for a walk."

I glanced at the laptop screen wistfully and then, stretching my arms above my head, I stood. "Yes, I think a walk would do me a world of good. Maybe it'll help me organize my thoughts." I slipped an arm around Caleb's waist and pulled him against my side. "Although, with you by my side, it's impossible to keep a clear head." He looked at me and gave me one of his heart-melting smiles. "See? I have no idea what I was thinking about a second ago. You're dangerous."

SURPRISES
EUREKA

"Can I open my eyes now?" Caleb had dragged me to a nearby town and made me walk with my eyes closed for at least a block. I had repeatedly crashed into walls and even people a couple of times. "I'm getting bruised all over."

"Stop whining. You can open them now." I opened my eyes to a nondescript gray door. *This is the surprise?* "It's what's inside, Sky, not the door."

Inside it was dark, and even my angelic eyes had trouble adjusting to the change from the sunshine outside. The walls were lined with drawings, sketches of many different types and colors. A rice paper wall separated a smaller room from the main one. Classical music wafted through the air as a tall, older woman came from behind the screen. "Good morning, Caleb. Is this the friend you told me about?"

I looked at Caleb and then back at the woman. "Am I the only one who doesn't know what's going on?"

"This is Celeste." Caleb put a hand behind my shoulders and pulled me gently closer to the woman. "She's an old friend of the family, and she's also the most amazing tattoo artist in the world."

Celeste laughed. I liked her laugh, open and honest. "Well, I don't know about the world, but I am pretty good."

Confused, I wrinkled my nose and combed my hair with my fingers. "I don't understand." Was this my swiss cheese brain playing tricks on me again?

Caleb slipped his arm around my shoulders. "I wanted to give you something special, and I thought you would like a tattoo." Now I was truly lost. What could I have ever said that made him believe I wanted a tattoo of all things? "Show him, Celeste."

The dark-haired woman stretched her arm and offered me a piece of paper. It was a drawing like the ones on the wall. My heart somersaulted when I realized what it depicted—a pair of beautiful wings. "They would be tattooed starting on your shoulder blades, moving into your upper arm, ending right before your elbow. I understand you have a special love for angel wings."

The sting of tears burned in my eyes. They weren't tears of sadness but of happiness. The knowledge that Caleb loved me enough to have thought of such an amazingly touching gift flooded me with a sense of joy. What had I done to deserve such love? I wiped the tears with the back of my hand.

"Do you hate it?" Caleb seemed worried, his face turning into a mask of doubt. "I'm sorry. I'm so stupid. What made me think this would be a good thing?"

I cupped his chin and kissed him, interrupting the stream

of self-doubt coming from his mouth. "I don't hate it, Caleb. I love it. I absolutely love it. Thank you." I hoped he knew I was thanking him for more than just the idea.

Celeste laughed. "I'm guessing you'll do it?"

By the time we went home a few hours later, I had the preliminary sketch of the wings drawn on my shoulders and arms. Celeste didn't act surprised or ask about the thin scars I had over my spine, what was left of my burned roots. I could no longer retract them, so they were both visible. Joan insisted on rubbing a scar ointment on it every day in hopes they would at least fade away. I liked them in a rather morbid way, a painful reminder of what had happened, but also a memorial of sorts for a part of me that I would never recover.

"How do you know Celeste?" I asked Caleb as we sat at the dinner table that night.

Joan perked up her ears. "Celeste? She's awesome." She took a large bite off the dinner roll. "I want her to give me a tattoo."

"You're not going to get a tattoo." Caleb gave her the don't-you-dare look.

"I'll be eighteen in less than a month. I'll get one if I so desire." Amusingly enough, Joan was picking up a lot of my language. "And if I want a fucking tattoo, I'll get the fucking thing." Then again, she hadn't lost any of her old language either.

"Oh my God, Joan." Caleb slammed his fork down on the plate. "Why can't you clean your filthy mouth? You talk like a sailor."

Joan took another bite of the buttered roll and mumbled, "Maybe I should join the Navy." I laughed quietly, afraid of pissing off Caleb. "Anyway, Sky, Celeste is an old family friend. She was one of my mom's patients."

Caleb's mom had been a therapist in Maine before her death. I had read it all in the files I had absconded from headquarters. "Isn't it unusual for a patient to get involved personally with the family of her therapist?"

"They were friends before their professional relationship." Caleb leaned back in his chair, hands behind his head. "She had a breakdown after she saw her husband of twenty years with another woman. She lost it and my mom came to her rescue."

Something in my brain clicked. Another woman. *Remember, remember.* Amy had always had a strange attachment to Gabriel, being the first one in the office and the last one to leave, always available for his every need and every request. *Why did I never see it?* Amy was in love with Gabriel. And he—

"I know why she did it!" I jumped out of my chair. Joan and Caleb looked at me as if I had grown a second head.

"Why she did what? And who's she?"

"I know why Cranky Amy made a pact with Samael." Of course! A woman scorned. Angels were no different. She had been "replaced" by whoever Gabriel had been dating. Amy must've snapped and decided to get back at him by framing him for a truly heinous crime. The fact that Caleb and I got caught in the crossfire was a bonus.

Both Caleb and Joan had stopped eating and exchanged

looks that clearly read "Oh crap! He's lost it!" I smiled, stupidly relieved for having figured out the mystery. I had told them the story from the beginning, about the note and my frustration at not having any idea who had planted it on Gabriel's desk for me to find it.

"But how did she achieve her goal by having you find the note? No one else knows about it, and the only people who got in trouble were you and me." Caleb had a point. If Amy's ultimate goal was to get back at Gabriel by disgracing him in the seraphic society, having me find it first wasn't the most brilliant move. "There has to be something else."

Silence fell as we all retreated into our own thoughts. "Who says she meant for you to find the note?" Joan's dark eyes shone as they always did when she had an idea.

I reached out and wrapped my arms around her neck. "You are brilliant, my elfin friend." She laughed and pretended to shoo me away. "She didn't know that Gabriel was going to send me to his desk to make a call. Amy fully expected the cleaning crew to find the note and report it to the upper echelon." I let go of her neck and pulled my phone from my pocket. "Gotta let Gabriel know."

He was beside himself with shock. At first he didn't want to believe me, but as I related everything I remembered, plus my findings on the surveillance video, he had no choice but to accept that he had been royally screwed by his most trusted.

"What I don't understand is why the cleaning crew or somebody else didn't find the note the next morning." I was baffled. "I left it in the same spot I had found it, in plain sight."

"I found it, you idiot." Well, the friendliness hadn't lasted long. "I came to work a lot earlier the next morning because I had left so early the day before and found the compromising note on the desk."

I was even more confused. "Then why ask me for help with the investigation? Couldn't you have done it more efficiently from headquarters?"

"Probably, but I wanted to have it done discreetly and distance myself from it as much as possible so as not to raise any suspicions." Gabriel sounded irritated. Admitting he had needed my help seemed to be as painful to him as swallowing shards of glass.

I couldn't resist. "I was the only one who could do it without being detected."

"Don't be cocky! It's very unbecoming."

Laughing under my breath, I winked at Joan, who was watching me with her big brown eyes opened wide. Gabriel thanked me in his usual dour manner, told me he would contact me later, and hung up on me.

"He's not coming over again, is he?" Joan placed the dirty dishes in the sink and put the kettle on for tea. "I just made another batch of cookies that I'll have to hide if he comes."

"Maybe he'll offer you a job baking cookies in Arcadia." I chuckled, pushing the chair in.

Caleb weaved his fingers on mine and pulled me to the couch. "Don't encourage her. She already has a giant head on those tiny shoulders of hers."

Joan stuck her tongue out at him from the kitchen.

The electric kettle began whistling. While the elfin girl busied herself brewing lavender tea for all of us, Caleb had nestled against me, his head on my shoulder. Our thighs were smashed together and our joined hands were lying on my lap. It felt like home, a feeling I didn't remember ever having throughout my very long life before I met the siblings.

My parents weren't exactly the warm kind. They had their jobs in different angelic squads, and when they came home at the end of their shifts, they didn't spend much time cuddling me in any way. Angels rarely did. I had always thought it strange that creatures who were made of love and whose mission was one of altruism and empathy could be so cold toward their own families and friends. It was almost as if love itself had lost its meaning amongst the seraphic beings and had become purely a job. Even as a tiny cherub, I'd wanted more. I wanted to experience the same kind of love I witnessed humans feeling toward each other. As a young one, I had often escaped unnoticed to watch couples sitting in the park, hand in hand, kissing or merely talking. The look in their eyes when they stared at each other was overwhelmingly beautiful. I wanted that.

Joan was the first one to go to bed. "I have a stupid algebra test tomorrow. Sky, what fucking angel decided that algebra was something all educated humans should learn? Or did that come from God himself?"

"Shit, Joan, you just uttered 'fucking' and 'God' in the same breath. Can you be any more blasphemous?" Caleb leaned forward, his elbows on his knees.

Ignoring her brother, Joan wiggled her fingers in a goodbye and slammed her bedroom door behind her. "And for fuck's sake, can you guys please go do it in your room, not in the living room?" Her voice came loud and clear through the door. Caleb choked and I laughed.

"She has no sense whatsoever." He seemed divided between being mad and amused. "If I didn't care so much for her, I would've throttled her a long time ago." He twisted around to look at me and I swear my insides liquefied. Those eyes had power.

"Thank you." It came out of nowhere and was one hundred percent sincere. I owed Caleb a debt I would never be able to repay. I owed him feelings and experiences I had only dreamed about. My angel heart had expanded with my love for him—and his sister as well. And my life… well, I may have lost my power to fly, but my life had a much richer texture now. Before Caleb, my days were a soft, beautiful, and shiny but rather uninteresting satin. Now my life was a richly colored brocade, full of intricate stitches and details, soft and rough all at the same time. I regretted nothing.

Caleb leaned back again, his side against mine and his hand resting across my middle. "What are you thanking me for? You're the one who rescued me from that evil angel." He lowered his voice an octave.

"But you, Caleb, saved me from a meaningless life." When had I become so cheesy? *Who cares?* I had this amazingly beautiful creature—inside and out—who loved me. I could afford to be as cheesy as I wanted. I doubted if Caleb cared either.

Straightening up on the couch, Caleb scooted a little and began pulling on the edges of my shirt. "Too many clothes."

I happened to agree. I suddenly had the overwhelming need to feel his skin against mine, every inch of his hard body touching mine. I helped him remove my shirt, and his followed. Our mouths met in a hungry, urgent kiss, but I couldn't help being scared. Now that the mystery had been solved, I would soon be recalled to Arcadia and away from my new family. Without my wings, I wouldn't be able to fly to Earth and visit. It may be a small eternity before I saw Caleb again, before I enjoyed his lovemaking—or it could be forever.

We got up and stumbled our way to the room, bodies entangled, arms in a frenzy, pulling and tugging. I didn't think I would survive without this anymore. This was my Heaven, in Caleb's arms. The door closed behind us and we fell noisily on the bed, our lips still connected, Caleb's hands behind my neck pressing my face against his. I wanted to swallow him whole, make him a part of me so no matter where I went, he would be with me always.

Caleb flipped me on my stomach and slowly, in a maddening caress, he studied the skin and muscles on my back with his hand. His fingers lingered first over my shriveled wings and then over the gorgeous lines of my future tattoo. "These are going to be beautiful, Sky. But not as beautiful as your real ones." The small circles he drew over my skin ignited a roaring fire, one I wasn't scared of, one I welcomed with open arms.

I turned onto my back. Caleb was kneeling at my side,

all lean muscle and sinew. I reached up and hooked my hands on his strong thighs, besieging him to come closer. He complied, the intensity in his eyes inducing a mad thumping in my heart. Grabbing hold of the elastic waist of my joggers, he began to peel them off me. Slowly, deliberately, and oh so arousing. When he followed his hands with his lips, I threw my head back in ecstasy and arched my hips against his mouth. My body tingled as if the stars in the heavens had all moved inside me. I wanted him to feel that too.

Swollen with desire, I pulled away just long enough to rid him of his pants. I sat at the edge of the bed with Caleb on my lap as I reached around his waist and began caressing him. He moaned and rubbed himself against my arousal. We sat like that for a while, touching each other, reveling in the other's reaction until we couldn't do it anymore. Caleb grabbed a condom, rolled it on himself, turned me around, and made me his again. We exploded in each other's arms, hysterically exhausted and happy, riding the waves of our mutual pleasure.

Later we lay side by side on his bed, a sheet over our lower halves and our sides still touching. Caleb turned suddenly and kissed my lips. "I love you, Sky. Say you'll stay forever."

My heart dropped a few inches. Of all the things he could've asked me, that was the one I couldn't promise. I was an angel. My life was not my own.

***

THE GIFT

The wing tattoo was almost finished. After a couple weeks of visits to the studio, Celeste was becoming a bit—well, a lot—suspicious of my strange and wondrous power of healing. "I've never seen anything like that," she said after my second and third visit. "You should still be raw in places, but it's totally and completely healed. I want some of whatever it is you eat, boy." We had stretched the time between visits after that. There was no hurry, after all.

Life had settled into a nice, easy-going rhythm. Caleb worked mostly from home so we could spend as much time as possible together. I hadn't said anything to him, but I think he knew that our time was coming to an end. It was tearing me up inside to even think of leaving him, but angels had very little choice. Sooner or later I would have to leave.

Joan's birthday was coming up, and she hoped—oh, who am I kidding? She demanded to be "surprised." "It's the big one-eight! I will officially be an adult and you, my prudish brother, will have no say as to how many 'fucks' I say, how many tattoos I get, or whom I date. It will be Nirvana." In her usual faster-than-light reasoning, she had immediately changed the subject to ask me, "Is that even a thing? Nirvana?"

I hoped it was, because I wanted to live there.

Gabriel had called a few times and even visited briefly to

check on me—or so he said. I suspected he was just making sure I stayed out of trouble. Maybe, because of Caleb's presence, he wasn't very forthcoming with information about Amy or Samael. He had promised that whatever contract Cranky Amy had signed with the dark side was now totally invalid. We could rest our minds at ease because neither Samael nor any of Asmodeus's favorites were interested in any of us anymore.

I still needed some closure for the sake of my wings. I also needed something, anything to make up for the fact that Caleb didn't remember me from our first time on the beach. We were together now, and we loved each other, but that had been that pivotal moment when I had broken through those unspoken and invisible angelic barriers in my heart and fallen in love with a human. A magnificent, sweet human. We had clicked, like Joan would've said. The second I looked into his lavender and green eyes, something had snapped inside of me, the chains that had held my heart captive for so long. I wanted him to remember that moment. I wanted to remember the instant I gave him my heart.

Winter was upon us. There was no more denying it. The air had the frosty quality that heralded the imminent arrival of snow. Caleb and I had walked to the waterfront, bought a couple of lobster rolls at Red's, and sat on a wooden bench at the pier, eating and watching the gulls soar above the cold water. I couldn't take my eyes off the birds as they flapped their wings and glided through the sky at great speeds. My eyes blurred as they filled with tears. Suddenly, my heart was bleeding with longing for my wings, for the feeling of the wind against my face—for something I could never have again.

Caleb's arm went around my shoulders. "I wish I could do something to make it better."

You already did. I wanted to tell him that, but my throat closed with the pressure of unshed tears. I leaned on him, enjoying the warmth and peace I always gathered from him, and wiped my eyes with the back of my hand. The blue of the waters and the call of the gulls soothed my soul, but my heart still ached. I had been the recipient of such blessings, my sweet Caleb and Joan. Ironically, the same blessings were also the cause of my heartache. As much as I tried not to think about it, I was getting more and more anxious about my approaching departure. I didn't know how to live without Caleb anymore. My life before him was a blur, a faded memory that I had no wish to go back to.

My phone rang. *What does Gabriel want now?* "Yes?" In no mood to talk to the one angel who in more than one way had been the involuntary catalyst to my misery, I braced myself for more of his hot air.

"Sky, I'm coming down to Earth to talk to you later today. Is that okay?" *Is Gabriel actually asking me for permission to do something? Am I dreaming?* I pinched myself to make sure I was awake.

"What was that?" Caleb asked as I put the phone away. I wasn't sure how to feel. Should I be worried? A terrible thought crossed my mind—was he coming to tell me it was time to go back? Instinctively, I tightened my hold on Caleb's arm. "What's wrong? Sky?"

"I don't want to leave you." It came out before I had time to stop myself. "I want to stay with you and Joan. You're my home now. I can't imagine living without you."

Caleb tilted his head in question. "What makes you think you're leaving? Did Gabriel say that?"

Tears rolled freely down my cheeks. "No, he didn't, but—"

Caleb didn't let me finish. He kissed my face, drinking up my tears and nibbling on my lips with such tenderness, such love, my bleeding heart rejoiced.

"I love you, and if keeping you here means I have to go head-to-head with a freaking archangel, that's what I'll do." He sounded so serious, I burst out laughing in spite of my pain. My tears, now on Caleb's tongue, carried a part of me—or so I hoped; a little part of me to remain within my lover's body after I left. Caleb joined me, chuckling in that funny way of his that made me feel all funny and fuzzy inside.

Gabriel didn't show up until after lunch. I was grateful Joan was still in school since I couldn't be sure my boss was bringing good news. In his best suit, Gabriel looked like any other human businessman. Had I not known of his seraphic origins, I would've never given him a second thought. His lips were stretched in a thin line, and I noticed he kept playing with his five-hundred-year ring—a gift from the big boss for years of good service.

Is he nervous?

We sat in the living room with a cup of coffee each. Caleb had offered him tea but Gabriel wasn't much of a tea person.

In fact, he may have appreciated a drop or two of bourbon in that mug.

"You wanted to talk to me, Gabriel. What's this all about?" *We might as well get this over with quickly. Do it like a Band-Aid and rip it off once and for all.*

Gabriel shot a glance at Caleb, as if uncomfortable having a human for a witness, but didn't ask him to leave. I chose to see that as progress of sorts. "Yes, there is something very important that I must talk to you about." *Uh-oh, here it comes.* He twisted the ring on his finger one more time. I had never known him to be so fidgety. "But first, I must extend Arcadia's most heartfelt apologies to Caleb for the terrible events that befell him at the hands of one of our brethren."

Oh geez! All the formality didn't bode well. He was obviously there on a very official capacity.

Caleb shifted uncomfortably in his seat and stole a glance toward me as if asking for help. I had no idea what was going on, so I shrugged and shook my head. "Of course, Gabriel. I don't hold you or your department responsible for any of what happened."

Way to go, my love. Hit him with the same formality.

Gabriel crossed and uncrossed his legs, played with his ring again, and forced a tiny smile onto his lips. "Thank you for saying that, Caleb. Unfortunately, I must assume part of the blame considering I failed to uncover the betrayal and wicked plotting from one of my own staff. But I do appreciate your sentiments. After long conversations with Father, I want you to rest assured that no seraphic creature will bother you again for many years to come."

I perked up at that. Was he saying that Caleb was going to be allowed to live a long life?

When Gabriel turned to me, my first instinct was to run and hide. Maybe dig up a giant hole right there in the living room and bury myself far, far away from the surface. No such luck.

"As for you, young Sky, I have also had long debates with Father about you and your role in all this." He had been discussing me with the big boss. I was in so much trouble. "I must first reprimand you on your totally unangelic decision to save a human from his predestined death." Shit. I hoped Caleb didn't catch that. I had yet to reveal the real reason I'd met him. "That went completely away from every seraphic directive, and it is punishable by law, as you know."

I cringed. Had I not been punished enough already?

Caleb looked nervous suddenly. "What do you mean 'punishable by law'?"

"Sky broke one of the main laws of angels." Gabriel's voice had that hard edge he often reserved for when he was chiding me about something. "Like with Earthbound humans, when an angel breaks the law, he gets punished." Caleb opened his mouth to say something, but Gabriel cut him off. "However." The emphasis on the word couldn't be missed. "He did atone for it with his desk job for a few weeks, and he has suffered more than anything the board of seraphic justice would ever impose on any law-breaking angel, so it was decided to let it go." I let out the breath I had been holding. "Sky, your debt to the justice system has been fully paid."

Caleb reached out for my hand and squeezed it, his heartwarming smile back on his face. Gabriel wasn't finished though; I could read his body language as well as I could read English.

"Father and I also discussed your…." He paused, searching for words. "We discussed your disability and came to a consensus. Obviously, you won't be able to serve in the death squad anymore." The fact that his words rang true didn't make them any easier to hear. "In fact, without your wings, young Sky, the only jobs you will be able to perform in Arcadia are desk jobs."

For once I didn't care. Even if they had given me back my squad job, I would've been torn away from the one I loved. My life was over one way or another, so a stupid job wouldn't make a difference. "I understand." It was merely a whisper, and I wasn't even sure Gabriel had heard it.

"In spite of your earlier misbehavior, you have proven to be…." Again that pregnant pause, as if he couldn't quite decide on what terms to use. "Worthy and courageous." I almost fell off my perch on the couch. Those were not words Gabriel had ever used when speaking about me. "Father and I agree that you have shown to be in possession of a true angelic heart. Your capacity to love is—unfortunately for us as a race who was created for the sole purpose of loving— unmatched in Arcadia these days. You were not only willing to defy orders from above and face the consequences of such an act, but also willing to suffer unspeakable pain in order to protect the one you love."

Heat climbed up to my face. Compliments weren't something I was used to, and coming from Gabriel, of all angels, wasn't settling well with me. "Thank you—I think." I sounded like a babbling idiot, not certain of what to say or how to act in the face of such rare praise. Caleb offered me a brilliant smile, and my muscles relaxed just a little.

"Such love and courage can't go unnoticed or unrewarded." Gabriel leaned forward, his elbows resting on his knees, and the first friendly glint I had ever seen showed in his eyes. "We decided, should you agree, that you shall be allowed to live among the humans for as long as you see fit."

Shock didn't even begin to describe what I felt. I was paralyzed. My brain was stuck in Park, and my voice wasn't working.

Caleb squeezed my hand, and I could've sworn he uttered a quiet hoot. "What do you mean?" I asked stupidly. My mouth was slack, and my heart might've stopped beating for a moment.

"Hell and tarnation, Sky." Gabriel's patience for me had apparently run out. "Don't be stupid. I'm telling you that you can stay on Earth with your humans for as long as you want. It's not like you'd be any help in Arcadia. Wingless and love-sick? Not a good combination for someone like you." I heard the word "liability" even if he didn't really say it. I didn't care anymore; he was offering me the one thing I wanted the most.

I glanced at Caleb, who was still holding my hand as a lifeline. There was a question in his eyes. How could he even doubt that was what I wanted? "Are you serious, Gabriel? You're okay with that?"

Gabriel stood up, obviously done with me and my doubts. "Yes, Sky. It's very okay with me." He enunciated the words as if he were speaking to an idiot—which he probably thought I was. "Stay here with your human boyfriend and be happy. Call me if you need anything." The look he gave me told me "don't call me, ever." I doubted I would anyway. I was perfectly fine with the idea of never having to see the archangel again.

As usual, my stoic boss left in a whirlwind of wavering air. Caleb and I were standing, our hands still connected. I was afraid of letting go and finding out that I had been dreaming. "This is real, right, Caleb? Gabriel really told me I could stay here with you."

Caleb reached out to me with his other hand and caressed my face. "Yes, this is real. If that's really what you want, of course."

I leaned in against his hand and its comforting heat. "It's what I've been dreaming about for the past few months. Do you want me to stay? I understand if you don't. If you think it's all too much to digest."

His lips sought mine, and I had my answer. My wings were gone, but I was still able to soar.

* * *

MEMORIES

"How do you like it?" Caleb and I were standing in Celeste's studio, my bare back turned to the big wall mirror as I stared at my new tattooed wings. They were a work of art, drawn in meticulous detail. Nothing could replace my real wings, but these were an amazingly beautiful memorial in their honor.

I smiled at the older woman in response.

"I'm still in awe of how quickly you heal, young one. I think I'm in love with my own work." She laughed.

"They're perfect, Celeste. Thank you." I held her hand and kissed her cheek. "I'm so very grateful to you."

"I'm grateful to you for letting my creative juices flow freely. One can get pretty bored drawing butterflies and dragons."

Caleb came to stand behind me and brushed a hand across one side of the wings, making me shiver in delight. "Sexy." It was a whisper for my ears only, but I saw Celeste's lips curl in a smile.

It was Joan's birthday, and we had to run the last errands in preparation for her "surprise." She was quite partial to the cakes at a Boothbay Harbor bakery, so we were heading there to pick up her gift.

Caleb had never collected his motorcycle—two accidents in the space of a few weeks were too much even for a bike lover like him—so we took a taxi instead. Her party was in the evening, and we had a lot of time to kill. The town was half-deserted, like most tourist towns during the winter. A few locals loitered around or hurried to get their shopping done and back into the warmth of their houses. The air was frigid, and I could almost smell snow in the air. It wouldn't be long now.

We chose a small cafe and sat in a booth where we could talk and hold hands away from prying ears and eyes. We hadn't talked about what Gabriel's decision really meant for us in the long run. Both of us were so happy with the news, we never once stopped to iron out the kinks. And there were some.

"You know I'll live a very long life and won't get old at the same speed you do." We sat cradling the hot mugs of tea the waitress had brought us. "Will you be all right with that?"

Caleb tapped a finger on his face and pretended to think. "Hmm, let me see. I'll be old and wrinkly and have a hot young man to keep me warm at night. Yes, I can see the hardship. However, I love you enough that I think I'll be able to handle it." I laughed and he kissed my knuckles, his gorgeous eyes never leaving mine. "I love you, fool. I don't care what you or I look like. I want you by my side. Forever."

He glanced around the mostly empty cafe, then brought his lips down on mine for a long, tantalizing kiss. "I want to kiss you like this a thousand times a day, slide my hands along your body, and make love to you every night." His hand had surreptitiously found its way to my thigh under the table. "Are you up for that?"

I was most certainly up for that and so much more. Caleb could make me feel like I owned the world. When I was in his arms, I forgot who I was and where I came from. I was just Sky, an average, half-broken person Caleb had saved with the power of a simple glance.

"You never told me how and why you came to my door that night." There it was, the question I had been dreading almost the whole time I'd been with him. How could I tell the one I loved that I'd been sent to harvest his soul? "And what was all that about you breaking the law and being punished? What law did you break, and when?"

There was no escaping now. "You know I am—I was—an angel of death, right?" He nodded. "My job was to harvest the souls of those who had died. We get a mission note and go meet the human who's about to depart this life. That day, I was coming for you, Caleb." His hand fell off my leg and his mouth went slack. "I didn't want to tell you, but you were slotted to die the first time I met you."

"When you came to the house?" I could see his Adam's apple bobbing up and down as he swallowed hard and frequently.

"No, I had met you before. You just don't remember." I scooted closer to him in the booth, placing my hand behind his shoulders. "The first time I laid eyes on you, I was hooked, bewitched, whatever you want to call it. I had come to harvest your soul and instead you harvested mine. I fell in love so hard I didn't even think twice. Instead of letting you die and then picking up your Heaven-bound soul, I prevented your death. Big bad violation of angelic directives."

"Was that my first bike accident?" I nodded, looking for

signs on his face that he wasn't mad at me. "But I thought I miraculously rolled off the bike before the semi crushed it to smithereens."

"I pulled you out before that." My fingers, entwined in his short hair, were shaking, half in nerves, half in yearning.

"I don't remember any of it. How can I not?" He sounded outraged by his own lack of memory.

I kissed him, pulling on his lower lip gently with my teeth. "It's not your fault. Gabriel has his magic too."

It was getting very hot in that little cafe, in the middle of a cold winter day. I wanted to lay Caleb across that table and explore his body again with my hands and my mouth. Being close to him was like having a constant fever that overtook my senses and made me crazy with desire.

"Why did you come back, then?"

Fool! Isn't it obvious?

"Because I was in love with you and I just couldn't not see you." Our mouths melded together again, his tongue prying its way between my lips and playing havoc with my senses. "You aren't very forgettable, you know."

Underneath the table, I slipped my hand farther up his thigh and smiled. He was as aroused as I was. I cocked my head to the side. "There's a nice little hotel around the corner. We have time."

Before we knew it, I had him pinned to the wall of the quaint hotel room, stark naked and burning with desire. I loved every inch of his handsome, lean body, and I made sure he knew I did. I caressed, licked, and kissed him from his eyelids to the most sensitive part of his body. His hands, splayed across my chest, fueled the fire roaring inside of me. I grabbed hold of one and guided it down my abs, then lower still until I could feel the heat of his palm against my arousal. Even now I was still surprised by the feelings this human could evoke within my body and soul. I didn't think I would ever get tired of it.

I turned him around to face the wall and felt the taut muscles of his chest and abs. Unable to control myself any longer, I rubbed my lower body against his and nearly exploded. Caleb pressed his backside against me, and I barely had time to pull out the condom and slip it on before I sank myself into him. We moaned loudly at the same time, and Caleb pressed himself even closer to me. My body spasmed in waves of pleasure, leaving me breathless. Still panting, I caressed Caleb until he joined me, his body shaking in climax. Still connected, we slid all the way to the floor and curled around each other, not wanting to break apart. We were one, body and soul.

The clerk at the hotel looked at us with a dirty smile as we checked out less than two hours later. We didn't care. He could think what he wanted; that was his privilege. Our love was pure and wholesome, and I was walking on air.

The bakery was down the street, but the cake wasn't ready yet. "What do we do now?" Caleb asked, looking at his watch. "Do we go back to the hotel and give the dirty-minded clerk something more to talk about?"

I laughed just as Caleb's phone rang. It was Joan.

"Where the fuck are you guys?" I could hear her voice

from the other end. Caleb shook his head. "Everybody's waiting for you."

"Joan, we're waiting for your cake. You know, the one you wouldn't compromise on?" Her precise words had been "No way in hell will I accept any cake from any other fucking bakery." Joan could be very persuasive when she chose to.

"Well, I'm hungry, and so are the guests." I heard her yell something, probably to said guests.

"Grab something from the fridge. God knows I bought enough food to feed an army." Caleb had the phone slightly away from his ear so I could hear his sister. "Why are the guests already there, anyway? They weren't supposed to come around until after eight."

"I called them all and told them to come earlier." Of course she did. "I was lonely with you lovebirds making googly eyes and unable to take your hands off each other."

"Boohoo." Caleb made a face at the phone as if Joan could see him. "Now you have to wait. Just feed the crowd before they turn on you and eat you." He hung up, laughing. "My sister. I swear she's crazier than a loon."

The cake wouldn't be ready for another hour, so we decided to walk on the beach. The air was freezing our breath as we strolled hand in hand along the shores of the harbor. I had been so distracted by Caleb's account of some of Joan's crazy tirades of the past that I hadn't realized we were walking on the same exact beach where we had met for the first time. The same sand I had crashed into after a mad plunge to Earth, knocking myself out. My breath caught in my throat as I spotted the rock where we sat and kissed for the very first time.

Unaware of the turmoil inside my heart, Caleb kept talking, his thumb caressing the top of my hand distractedly. When I stopped abruptly in front of the rock, it took him a few seconds to notice the change in pace.

"Can we sit for a second?" I asked, tears threatening to pour out.

We sat on the cold rock, the icy temperature seeping through my clothes and into my skin. Caleb looked around, staring out into the bay, eyes faraway. "This feels familiar." My heart thumped. "I know I've been here many times, but I mean this, here with you, feels so right."

My hand went around his waist and pulled his warm body closer to mine. "Yes, it does." What could I say? *"This is where our lips met for the very first time?" "This is where I saw your lavender field eyes and fell head over heels in love with you?"* I wanted him to remember, but not because I was placing those memories there by telling him what happened. I wanted him to remember because he felt as strong a pull as I did.

"What were you doing the first day we met?" My eyes opened wide. "I mean, before you came to collect my soul. What were you doing?"

I chuckled. "What I always did: flying free-form as fast as I could, all the way down." A shiver went through me at the memory of the feeling the crazy speeds always brought me. "I'm not really liked by the other angels. I'm the weird one, the one who enjoyed doing things other angels couldn't care less for. Gabriel calls me the 'liability.'" I laughed. It didn't feel so bad now that I was with my love. "Were you weird in school?"

"No, I was one of the cool ones." He wasn't being cocky; I could tell it was a plain, simple fact. "I already drove a motorcycle, and I guess that made me cool in the eyes of everybody else." His voice went down to a somber whisper. "But when my parents died in that accident, I withdrew from everything and everyone. I had Joan to take care of. She was just a kid, and I was the only family she had left."

I had read his file, from his C-section birth in nearby Portland through the traumatic years following his parents' death. He had gone from being a young man without many cares to the one responsible for bringing up a school-age sister. Gone were the parties, the haunting of bars at night, the wild hookups with strangers. Overnight he had become an adult and shut off his youth.

"I'm sorry about your parents. I'm sure they went to a good place."

Caleb turned his face and kissed me on my cheek. "It's in the past, and the future is looking very bright." Our lips fused again. When we separated, Caleb's eyes shone like stars in the night sky. "Kiss me again."

I obliged, sweeping my tongue over his lips slowly and then thrusting it into his mouth, exploring and tasting the honeyed tartness of him.

He blinked his out-of-focus eyes and licked his lips as if trying to place the flavor I left behind. "I remember." It was so sudden, I almost jumped off the rock.

"Remember what?" I was afraid of hoping for the impossible.

"It was here, on this same rock." My heart flipped a couple times. "You had crash-landed on the beach, and my friends and I found you unconscious by the shore. I remember thinking I must've been dreaming, but my friends saw you too, a creature of beauty and light."

I began crying. First it was just a soft whimpering that I doubted Caleb heard, but it became more intense as he continued his story. "My friends left and we sat on this rock. I knew you were an angel as soon as I saw you. When you unfurled your wings and sheltered us from outside eyes, I thought I might have died and gone to Heaven. But I wasn't there yet. Your lips took me there."

Crying in earnest, I wrapped my arms around him. "You don't know how happy you made me by remembering. Gabriel erased your memory of me, of our first meeting."

He caressed my head, then buried his fingers in my curls. "Was that the day I was supposed to die?" I went stiff against him. I didn't want him to remember that. Not that part. I couldn't lie to him though, so I nodded. "Ironic, don't you think?"

I pulled away so I could look into his eyes. "What do you mean?"

He smiled then, that beautiful, pure smile that stretched from his lips to his eyes. "Instead of dying that day, I started living again."

ACKNOWLEDGEMENTS

A heartful thank you to my amazing NVWP writing group whose gasps of surprise, sighs, and encouraging words over the first scene of *Lavender Fields* motivated me to write this special romance. A very special thank you to Katlyn who beta read the novel.

A huge note of gratitude to my readers past, present, and future. You make my job as a writer so very rewarding.

As always, many thanks to Hot Tree Publishing for believing in my stories and supporting me all the way. A big heart-you to the kick-ass women at Hot Tree (staff and authors) who are amazing and a second family of sorts. You ladies rock!

My fabulous editor Jonathan from iFlow Creative, who has been lending me a hand since book one. He's a great cheerleader—without the pom-poms.

My husband who does not understand my love for fiction but indulges me nevertheless. Thank you for your patience and support.

My son Christopher whose passion for weather mirrors my passion for writing.

My mom and dad for always encouraging me to follow my dreams. My sister for being my best friend forever and whose love for angel lore is sure to have inspired me to write Sky.

And my son Kyle who dreams of finding the love of his life and getting his own happily ever after. This is for you.

ABOUT THE AUTHOR

Natalina wrote her first romance in collaboration with her best friend at the age of 13. Since then she has ventured into other genres, but romance is first and foremost in almost everything she writes. Her novel, We Will Always Have the Closet, is her first published romance.

After earning a degree in tourism and foreign languages, she worked as a tourist guide in her native country, Portugal, for a short time before moving to the United States. She's lived in three continents and a few islands, and her knack for languages and linguistics led her to a master's degree in education. She lives in Virginia where she has taught English as a second language to elementary school children for more years than she cares to admit.

Natalina doesn't believe you can have too many books or too much coffee. Art and dance make her happy and she is pretty sure she could survive on lobster and bananas alone. When she is not writing or stressing over lesson plans, she shares her life with her husband and two adult sons.

You can reach out to Natalina at the following places:

Facebook: WWW.FACEBOOK.COM/AUTHORNATALINAREIS

Website: WWW.CATARINADEOBIDOS.WORDPRESS.COM

Twitter: WWW.TWITTER.COM/TichaB

ABOUT THE PUBLISHER

Hot Tree Publishing opened its doors in 2015 with an aspiration to bring quality fiction to the world of readers. With the initial focus on romance and a wide spread of romance sub-genres, we envision opening up to alternative genres in the near future.

Firmly seated in the industry as a leading editing provider to independent authors and small publishing houses, Hot Tree Publishing is the sister company to Hot Tree Editing, founded in 2012. Having established in-house editing and promotions, plus having a well-respected market presence, Hot Tree Publishing endeavors to be a leader in bringing quality stories to the world of readers.

Interested in discovering more amazing reads brought to you by Hot Tree Publishing or perhaps you're interested in submitting a manuscript and joining the HTPubs family? Either way, head over to the website for information:

WWW.HOTTREEPUBLISHING.COM